The Eye of Mayenga

Jaspher Rori

Nsemia

First Edition: May 2013
Published by Nsemia Inc. Publishers (www.nsemia.com); Oakville, Ontario, Canada

Edited By: Sheena Brennan
Cover Concept & Illustration: Jaspher Rori
Cover Design: Danielle Pitt
Layout Design: Kemunto Matunda

Note for Librarians:
A cataloguing record for this book is available from Library and Archives Canada.

ISBN: 978-1-926906-30-0

DEDICATION

I dedicate this book to my dear sisters, Mary Nyang'ate Arap Chuma, Hellen Moige Nyabotobe Mose and Jane Nyekerario Nyachoti; and the songs herein to my dear parents, Agnes Moraa and James Rori. The large age gap in between you and me count nothing as we are kindred spirits with a complete unity of purpose. You held me high, sang me lullabies, and taught me the virtues of love and purpose in life.

Acknowledgements

An idea cropped up in my mind one evening and by the next morning, it had developed into a skeleton. I had little material and creative energy, but I needed meat and juice to spice it, and when I shared my intentions to a few friends, they added fire. "That is a great idea." And I lit a candle, pieced the sentences into a paragraph and so on.

I'm grateful to all those who have morally and materially contributed to the writing of this work and its eventual publication. The Gusii people may agree with me that it's not necessary to fetch water from the fall, *egetogomera,* and carry it uphill, when the same water has its source uphill. I cite Ruth Sarange, Shem Abere, Ibrahim Mosoba, Janet Mokeira, Simion and Cecilia Morendi, Edna and Evans Chacha, Jackline, Joseck Nyantino, George Nyaberi (Ph.D.),Yona Sakatcha (UoN), Joseph Awino (UoN), and Duke Mose for their moral support during the writing of this book. I note the contributions of Mrs Kuria, my English/Literature teacher, and my classmates; Moi Forces Academy, Nairobi, 1987, for their sturdy grasp and interest in literature. I note the role played by Dados Hotel, Kisii, during the writing of this book. Lastly, I acknowledge the role played by Journalist Jimmy Achira, the author of *"Mwakenya: Real or Phantom? - A Journalist's Harrowing Experiences in the Moi Regime,"* for having encouraged me to complete this work and for his efforts to introduce me to the publisher who received my work over-readily.

Last, but not least, I pay my glowing tribute to Dr.

Matunda Nyanchama, the publisher of *Nsemia Inc. Publishers,* Ontario, a Canadian-based publishing firm, for receiving my work and agreeing to publish it.

About the Author

Jaspher Rori was born in West Mugirango, Nyamira County, Kenya. He attended Moi Forces Academy for Ordinary and Advanced level, and the University of Nairobi where he graduated with a B.Sc. degree in Agriculture. He also has a Diploma in project Management from Kenya Institute of Management. Presently, he is enrolled in post-graduate studies in Project Planning and Management at the University of Nairobi. Currently, he doubles as a part-time lecturer at the University of Nairobi.

Jaspher has worked as a high school teacher and as a manager in the tea industry in Kenya. He likes writing on a number of themes with a special interest in Gusii history, proverbs and sayings. He credits his passion to his parents and grandparents who were keen storytellers with many of these tales shared in evening fireside chats.

He is the author of A Beacon of Hope; (2011, Nsemia. Inc. Publishers, Ontario, Canada.) He is currently working on *Gusii History, Culture, Proverbs and Sayings*. In addition, he is writing a book of short stories tentatively titled *The Forces of Nature*.

Foreword

The Eye of Mayenga brings out challenges of rural African communities at a cross roads between tradition and modernity; the village of Mayenga is a replica of this society. Although the village is rich in culture and resources, lethargy and apathy are pronounced, perhaps because it has been sheltered from world trends and realities. The village of Mayenga lacks purpose; there is no evidence of mission and vision. Stuck in traditional beliefs, residents seem to be perpetually partaking in cheap illicit liquor; and life is punctuated by petty gossip and pessimisms – factors counterproductive to development – resulting in a spiral web of uncertainties.

This myriad of challenges is seen by Vincent Senta who has acquired a modern education, is well exposed and willingly carries the burden of agent of change for Mayenga. He successfully mobilizes and organizes a women's group and initiates an eye-catching water project whose fame reverberates across the county. Mayenga for once starts to see the need for change. However, trifling gossip and a troubled family life take their toll on Senta. To escape the harsh reality, he finds solace in an amoral relationship with his secretary through which he contracts the HIV virus to which he succumbs a few years later. Despite the medical exposition and advice on the disease, his death is blamed on his hard-to-understand neighbours who live in solitude because of their faith. The village of Mayenga strongly believes the neighbours bewitched Senta. And in a revenge mission, the neighbours are burned alive in broad daylight as the local chief helplessly watches. Though rumours were rife that the neighbours carried the cross of Senta's death, nobody had answers to the chief's torrential questions: Who? When? Why? What? and How?

The book underscores the role of education in management and leadership. It further provides an insight into the role of projects in community development and the challenges these projects encounter in the process of identification and final implementation.

Further, the author brings out sociopolitical and economic challenges facing a multitude of societies, including negative religion that could negatively impact development.

Apart from being an excellent story to read, it is a commendable book for students in community development.

Joseph A. Awino, Lecturer University of Nairobi

Chapter One

The morning sun successfully surged in from the east, but the leeward part of Mayenga was still smoky and misty. Birds cheerfully chirped and sang dirges from their nests. It was a chilly and a windy morning. Areba whistled and sang elegies in a soulful voice as he flashed his fly whisk in the wee air. His eyes were sore and red. He hadn't slept a wink the whole night. He wore the same clothing he had worn the previous day and enthusiastically moved his head left and right with each composed whistle. Occasionally, he stopped to blow his nose and wipe it with the back of his hand, and then reach for his tobacco sniff from a little black container in his overcoat, scoop it, sniff and squeeze his nostrils tight for the stuff to take effect.

He jigged and paced outside the house of his first born son, Vincent Senta. It was a modern red-brick house, with a red gal-sheet roof and navy blue mounted steel doors and windows. On the upper side was his house, built in the same design. Senta had built it for him and his wife Nyaboe, and these were the only "permanent" houses in Mayenga village. This was Senta's first venture as he entered his practice as a lawyer. Senta had aggressively established his law firm: Vincent Senta & Company when he began advocating in Nairobi, five years after graduating from law school. His effort to transform Mayenga had earned him a name, and he was seen as an icon of the village by the young and the old.

There was a three-legged stool decorated with beads and cowry shells and several wooden chairs arranged in an iron-roofed shade outside Senta's house. A log of fire simmered, though weakly, in the shade, evidence that people had spent the night there. The villagers took turns spending the night with the Senta's family, to comfort and keep the family warm and "brave" at these moments of trial. From inside the house, a lonely radio player belted soulful songs one after the other. As he jigged, Areba whistled and sang repeatedly, drowning out the voice on the radio. The songs and the whistles were expressively soulful and were a reflection of a man whose spirit was distraught with life:

> *Genda morangeri Gwako*
> *Gwako nyamosira mororo*
> *Gwako nyamosira mororo*
> *Gwako tamanyeti koroga*
> *Gwako n'omosira amanyete*
> *Gwako nyasira mororo*
> *Gwako nyamote mororo*
>
> *Gwako ee Gwako*
> *Gwako ee Gwako*

Translated as:-

Go and fetch Gwako
Gwako the tough medicine man
Gwako the tough medicine man
Gwako does not know how to bewitch
Gwako knows only how to uncast witches

Gwako the tough medicine man
Gwako the tough medicine man
Gwako ee Gwako
Gwako ee Gwako

Everyone in the village of Mayenga now believed that Vincent Senta was a victim of first-class witchcraft. He had defied all modern and conventional medicines (herbs). He had been taken to all local health centres and leading hospitals (Russia Hospital in Kisumu and Kenyatta Referral Hospital in the capital city), and he had been treated by the most qualified doctors in the land, to no avail. His condition had worsened with the dawn of each day. Gwako, the renowned and tough medicine man, was now seen as the only solution to his illness.

Areba had visited a diviner, Ongwacho, at night. He did not want people to know of his visit lest the evil ones crying with him by day, but tormenting his son by night, outsmarted him with an even tougher spell. Ongwacho had laid out the tools of his trade: an old python skin, cowry shells from the ocean and several rudimentary objects. He had confirmed Areba's greatest fear, that Senta, his first-born son, was indeed a victim of first-class witchcraft.

Ongwacho was undeniably known beyond the village. He was only good in divinations, not in treatment of illnesses. However, he could direct one to a medicine man who could treat and cure his son. He had contacted Keronche, who Senta's mother, Nyaboe, and aunt Moige had visited earlier to seek divination. Ongwacho had told them that as a child, Nyaboe had mistakenly seen a path of a python as she fetched firewood in a forest. Indeed the irate spirits of the beast, he said, had followed her long after into her matrimonial home and were now responsible for her son's illness. Had she known it in time, he alleged, she should have named Senta, Basweti, after the python, to put the wrath of the serpent to respite. Nevertheless, she urgently needed to appease the spirits of the offended python for Senta to heal. For this divination alone, Areba parted with ten thousand shillings, an equivalent of two goats.

Although Nyaboe could not recall seeing a path of a python as she grew up fetching firewood in forests near her paternal home, to appease the spirits of the offended reptile, Areba sacrificed a white bull by the river as directed, and let its blood flow into the waters downstream. It was done in the evening as the sun was going down, for there was a belief that the spirits came out at such a time to roam and look for food. The bull's head was first covered with a python skin, cursed in with a mock ceremony to inhale the incensed spirits of the reptile before the bull's life was snuffed out through suffocation and breaking its neck. Finally, the bull was slaughtered. It was important that it was a white bull; white was associated to cleansing and hence a white bull, slaughtered in this manner, would clean the homestead. Some meat from the bull was roasted and eaten by those present. The rest was hung on nearby tree branches for the roaming spirits of the python and other beasts of the jungle to eat, thus vanquishing and eliminating the tormenting spirits. No meat was taken home lest the ritual would fail in its effect.

The instructions were followed with great precision and Vincent Senta was renamed Basweti that same evening. But Vincent did not heal. Instead, his health worsened each day. He coughed continually, producing a thick and blackish mix of mucous and blood. He had a high fever and his body dripped sweat like a marathon runner. He lost his appetite, weight and became too frail to even move himself in bed.

The elders now agreed that Gwako could be the only solution. One had to be given "legs and a tongue" to fetch him as he was in high demand all over the land. This included bus fare and a convincing tongue to quicken his steps before it was too late. Mayaka, Senta's age mate, had to forgo his duties as a teacher to fetch the medicine man. An impromptu fundraiser was held to quicken Mayaka's legs and oil his tongue. They raised enough money to enable Mayaka to go and look for Gwako. Immediately, he set out to the village of Bombi, Gwako's home several ridges away.

Gwako's fame reverberated beyond the county of Gusii. He was reputed to cure with the powers of spirits any form of witchcraft and ailment which had defied conventional herbs or *mete anchogu*. However, one had to be prepared to part with several cows depending on what the spirits demanded. Gwako had no problem. People knew him as a good man, respectable and with a benevolent heart. But his tools of trade, among them the spirits from the waters, the scary hills and the skies, could demand anything depending on the nature and seriousness of the illness. Gwako, as their faithful messenger, would haplessly convey the message and plead for his clients. Sometimes the spirits were fair, and sometimes they were not. Only

Gwako had the power to communicate and plead with them when they appeared unreasonable. Most of the payments therefore went to the spirits. He only received a little for the "stomach and the forest." He often made long journeys to forests and travelled to far-off places to obtain his medicine and rejuvenate his prowess. It was necessary that those trips and his stomach were catered for by his clients.

Gwako was an irresistible character in the village of Bombi where he was born and lived. He was gifted in making people laugh, cry, angry, sad, and then laugh again. He gave hope to his clients even before he set the tools of his trade to start his work. Gwako said that he could not close his eyes to the suffering of the people he loved. He saw a thousand ways of solving miseries, with the powers of the spirits, afflicting people he was believed to treasure and to serve so earnestly. Many opted to be cured by him rather than go to hospitals where medicine and treatment were beyond reach. Yet, Gwako could heal in three-piece treatments through divination and with the powers of the spirits and local herbs, *mete anchogu.*

In the past, Gwako had solved many miseries and unearthed many disturbing riddles. He foretold the future. "If you don't plant now, you will have no food," he would advise a recovering patient. "These seeds here on your palm will multiply sevenfold in your garden and you will be richer than those who envy you. They will tremble in fear before your eyes." When it took too long to rain, he led the people into prayers giving them hope that soon it would rain. And somehow, it rained. It was not strange how Gwako knew what went on in people's lives, and what would happen in the near future. Everybody knew that he communicated directly to the spirits of the skies, the waters and the scary hills, and the spirits earnestly listened only to him.

Gwako's other names were Elias and Bull. Elias was a name that cut his umbilical cord. He earned the name Bull, as he could hold any disease by the horns and cure it. Unfortunately, he was born with a hunchback, a condition that was an anathema. He walked around with a lurch and an elbow stoop with sustained effort. When he was born, he remained hidden by his parents in the hut until he accidentally crawled out on his own one morning to play with other children. His mother, who had concealed him out of shame, quickly returned him to the house. It was said in whispers that Gwako was conceived out of an incestuous relationship. By doing so, his mother had carried her own waste on her palms. And with Gwako's birth, nature had taken its share in a form of a curse and eventual punishment. She had to be chastised as she had violated the norms of the land. As Gwako had not wronged anybody and was only a victim of circumstances, he had found favour with the spirits, who wanted to extend their influence on the land. And so, through him an opportunity arose.

Nobody really had a true story about it, but it was whispered all around until it reached his mother, Muma's ears. To add salt to the wound, Gwako proceeded to cut his milk teeth from the upper cleft. This too was an abomination in the land. Children hardly cut their milk teeth from the upper cleft. Rare cases had a meaning and required urgent divination. He could neither play with other children lest he inflicted them with a bad omen, nor drink milk from neighbours' cows. The belief was that the lactating cows could go dry the next evening. So, Muma, logically, was a troubled woman and could not buy or get milk from her neighbours. She could not bear the extra shame of being labelled incestuous. To her, it confirmed that something was absolutely wrong with her family. Some spirits or ancestors were displeased with her and were out for revenge for reasons unknown. Alternatively, she believed that an evil eye was trailing her in Bombi to torment her. To escape from the troubles, Elias was secretly moved from the village at night by his parents to an unknown place, far away from the tormenting eyes and spirits. When the parents returned they offered a sacrifice of a white ram to cleanse their homestead. It was necessary they did so to ensure the future was clean and clear.

Nobody knew of the whereabouts of Gwako until twenty years later, as a grown-up, one morning Elias made his way to the village of Bombi, carrying with him an assortment of strange regalia. He staggered like a bush swaying in the wind, adorned with a python skin and a bead-dotted snake necklace. In one hand was a walking stick supporting his deformed, fragile legs, and in his muscular hand he held an old black bag.

Everybody ran away to a distance from where they stared at him like people watching a movie with worriment. Who in the village had dared touch these items except the dreaded medicine men? Elias beckoned them with a sarcastic confident but croaked laughter; laughter similar to howls of hyenas. "Don't runaway my kinsmen," he boomed in a croaked voice as he swayed in a stagger. "I'm Elias Gwako, son of

Tanda. But now, call me Gwako the bull. The young Elias who left the village as a baby with a hunchback has finally sniffed his way back to his roots," he boomed pointing to his back. "Look at my back. Can you believe it?"

Nobody recognised him except his mother. The hunchback spilled out memories of a young Elias. This time, he was not the young Elias Tanda. He was Gwako the bull. "I've come to serve you by the powers of the spirits of the scary hills, the waters and the skies. I'm as strong as a bull, and I can grab any situation and ailment by its horns," he croaked.

Slowly, the crowd swelled around him, albeit frightened. The young and the old alike stared at him in bewilderment. "Indeed it is him," the elders confirmed. Then, he led them in a long monologue. He talked in a language unfamiliar to them, calling the spirits to hear and listen to him, protect him, and lend a hand to serve his people.

His first miracle in Bombi was rain. That season there had so much rain that it filled the rivers and flooded the land. Previously, a whole planting season had gone to waste without a single drop of rain. Plants had withered. Animals and people were thirsty and hungry. Birds hardly sang. The soils were bare and cracking with winds carrying their grains in tandem to the air each time it blew. He preceded a patch of lonesome grey clouds which appeared the same evening in a dry sky. "I've smelled your tribulations. I've brought you the rains," he announced that evening as he pointed to the sky. "Look over there," he pointed to the grey clouds with his webbed palm. "You will plant your crops and no seed will die. Not a grain. Your animals will have enough grass and your stomachs will not rumble, but will be full once again," he assured the people.

Two days later, it rained with madness. Women collected water from the roofs of their houses until all the containers in the houses were full. Soils imbibed to their fill, the gaping gullies and valleys disappeared and the earth became muddy; rivers overflowed at their banks, and the entire landscape turned green again with bolting blossoms. Everybody knew that Elias had brought too much rain as a lesson for banishing him from the village at a tender age. Others said he had brought the rain to win them over. That indeed, he was more blessed than the able bodied persons. But there was too much, as it rained day and night unabated. People stayed indoors warming themselves around hearths till there were no more logs to sustain the fires. There were disquiet murmurs all over Bombi. "What's Elias doing to us? Is he punishing us? Send the elders to plead for us to hold back the rains," they implored.

Nobody knew whether the elders of Bombi approached him to plead on their behalf, but soon after, a strong wind started to blow southwards. Elias came out of his hut and roared pointing to the sky, "enough with the rains." Three days later, heavy rain clouds had congregated in the sky, but a rainbow superseded them. It did not rain. The rains slowly subsided, and people went into planting and weeding. His fame and respect spread far and wide. He was revered as a rainmaker and feared as a tough magician. People held him in awe. They called him Gwako and not Elias anymore as he had commanded.

Chapter Two

Gwako arrived at Mayenga that evening as the sky was rolling down, in the company of Mayaka. Mayaka had finally traced him in the heartland of Gombe village where he was exorcising licentious spirits of ancestors that had tormented a boy to madness. He had convincingly put his case as urgent, and Gwako had felt the urgency and quickly exorcised the spirits so that they could hasten their feet to Mayenga. They left Gombe as the boy was in a convulsive state, foaming from his mouth and nostrils. The spirits tormenting him were on their way out. Gwako had reassured the boy's family. He gave them seven days and the boy would be alright. But, before seven days, he instructed, they should have settled their debt with the spirits of the scary hills, the skies and waters to completely get a hold of the evil spirits tormenting the boy. "Two cows and a goat were all the indomitable spirits demanded," Gwako commanded.

They left Gombe as the boy's family was without delay consulting one another on how to raise the stipend of the unassailable spirits and a goat for Gwako, for his stomach and the forest.

"I have smelled a rat," Gwako firmly made his announcement in his croaked voice before a gathered crowd of villagers outside the house of Senta's parents. "Senta will be alright, but the evil and ruthless spirits have half-broken the back of the eye of Mayenga as I speak. However, with the powers of the spirits that I meticulously command, they have no chance to do more harm," he reassured the crowd. "They are now seething and shuddering in their cocoons in anger. They must piss to their last intestines." With urgency, he dictated as he paced in front of the crowd with a logical jauntiness. "We mustn't waste more time lest the full back breaks and is no more."

He proceeded to spread the tools of his trade on the ground in a meticulous manner, as the anxious crowd watched in trepidation. Among his tools were skins from a python and a leopard, an assortment of animal skulls and horns, old dirty rugs, bottles of black, green and red concoctions and several cowry shells, which he had fetched from his age-old black bag that appeared to have been made of hippopotamus skin. Then, he sat on a three-legged stool he had come with and proceeded with his divination.

"You have no powers over me, you crude evil ones," he shouted at the top of his voice trembling, using the language of the magicians and gazing to the sky. "I speak by the mighty powers of the indomitable spirits of the skies, the waters and the scary hills. You must piss out to the last of your intestines, you crude brutes." Then, he methodically fetched one of his longest horns from his bag and sniffed into it again gazing into the sky. Shortly, a live brown chameleon emerged from it, flipping its long red tongue and dotting its eyes quizzically. He held it up by the apex of its tail. The chameleon coiled back into the horn. "Can't you be ashamed little thing," he rebuked it as it obediently recoiled into the horn. And as if possessed, Gwako started to sweat. Beads of sweat appeared all over his face as he communicated to the spirits with zest. "Papa! Papa! The mighty ones of the waters, the skies and the scary hills. Come down quickly. Hasten your wings quickly as your servant has commanded you to do. Let your presence be felt among the people of Mayenga." He violently shook his two-beaded gourds.

However, when the spirits appeared to take longer to respond, he shook the gourds even more vigorously, this time haplessly pleading with them not to let him down. "I plead to you, the mighty ones. I shall take your demands this time. I know you ate nothing today as I pleaded for Gombe that they should settle their debt in seven days. But, you won't go hungry here," he beseeched. His face was wet and shiny.

The crowd was eagerly stunned. "I can hear you from afar as you converse," Gwako proceeded to announce the arrival of the spirits. "Come. Fly the way you do." Then he turned to the crowd clapping violently. "Welcome the spirits of the waters, the skies and the scary hills. Clap your hands and applaud them harder as the mighty ones arrive here."

The crowd proceeded to clap in earnest. Suddenly, Gwako's bag, on the floor in front of him, gradually began to vibrate. The crowd watched it shudder violently with the jingle of bells sounding from it. "The mighty ones are finally here," Gwako firmly made the announcement and then proceeded to communicate to them as the people held their breath in wonder.

"Doctor," a hoarse tired voice called from the vibrating and jingling bag. "We have no time to waste. We are hungry and tired."

"Yes, Papa," Gwako answered obediently.

"We can see the patient is very sick, and half of his back is broken by the crude ones," the voice informed. "We have already banished the spirits, but they will find their way back once we leave. They are guided to this home by hidden witches buried behind the house of the patient. They want blood, human blood, and this won't be the end of it. They are strong demons that found their way to the home from the waters where they are utterly harmless. We shall bind and cast them into the deep waters where they belong."

"Yes, Papa," Gwako affirmed nodding.

"One more thing, doctor," the voice decisively said. "Ensure you exorcise the hidden witches behind the patient's houses. They were put there by ones not in this midst to guide the spirits to the home."

"Name them the mighty ones," a section of the crowd roared back deafeningly.

"Shhhh! Quiet!" Gwako sternly croaked back. "The spirits only communicate to me, their servant. Not to ordinary people!"

Indeed, people regarded Gwako as a spirit. He was said to be half-human and half-spirit; human when dealing with people and a spirit when communicating with the spirits.

"Once the witches are exorcised, burned to ashes, and the ashes swept by the waters to the sea, these demons will lose track of the home," the voice continued. "It's not the business of the spirits to expose witchcraft in Mayenga, but a thorn that pricks you is within reach. The ones responsible are not in this meeting, but they share waters with the people of Mayenga. They are driven by innate and shrewd jealousy, and they are now seething in fear and invoking their powers not to be exposed and harmed," the voice convincingly informed. "They are powerless before us. That is why they can't dare be in our presence. In seven days," the voice assured, "the patient will be well, and back on his feet. Our pay is four cows and a goat. We shall drink the cows' blood in the sea, and the goat is for your stomach and legs, Doctor!" The voice echoed, "Any question before we leave?" the spirits forcefully inquired as they concluded.

"Papa. I plead for Mayenga. I know you are hungry and tired. Gombe is paying in two days' time. Mayenga has gone through a lot of turmoil in this. Four cows, Papa, will be too much. Make it less," Gwako earnestly pleaded.

"We have seen their suffering. That is why we hastened our wings. We shall now fly back slowly. We reduce them to three and a goat; one cow for the spirit of the hills, another for the sea, one for me, the spirit of the skies and a goat for your stomach and legs."

The crowd was immensely stunned of what they had seen and heard before them. Gwako was indeed a powerful spirit able to solve their afflictions. Momentarily, the bag began to vibrate again, and the jingles sounded louder in a crescendo and faded in a diminuendo. Then all was quiet as the sun set in a last peep. The spirits had flown away to the skies as the crowd was left holding their breath and with questions on their lips! Who are these witches? Who among the villagers drink the water of Mayenga and were not in the meeting? Who are these driven by instinctive jealousy and invoking their powers not to be exposed and harmed? It dawned on them that Mecha and his wife Moraa were the only ones from the village not in the meeting. As exclusively devout people in their faith, they had not attended Gwako's divination meeting when the horn was distinctively blown to call the villagers. They had nothing to do with divination, exorcism or with a village that had gone against the Almighty Almighty.

Shortly after, noise of drums, songs, claps and incessant prayers were heard from Mecha's house, invoking the Almighty Almighty to take control and the devil, *nyachieni,* to be cast in fire. It was a confirmation of Gwako's divination, that indeed, they were responsible for Senta's ailment. Gwako had only hinted, "The ones responsible are not in this meeting, but they share waters with the people of Mayenga."

Hastily, three cows and a goat were driven out of the kraal and paid before Gwako exorcised the witches hidden behind Senta's house. It was a startling and a shameful sight. Pieces of the rotting clothes Senta wore as a child, soils of his footsteps, his spit, his books, his money and assortment of dead preserved animal bones and skulls were all wrapped together in a tight black polythene sheet. They were bound by crude spirits and cursed to torment Senta to his grave, Gwako informed the crowd as he unwrapped and displayed them.

"Why did he build such a house in the village where there are so many evil eyes?" Gwako wondered loudly as he keenly stared towards the "witches."

"The evil ones in your midst don't want him to prosper. All they want of him is misery!" He methodically put the "witches" in an old crucible and burnt them before the stunned elders, then he prescribed concoctions of magic wands and herbs before he left with the ashes and the tools of his trade into the dark night, all alone. He was a spirit, it was believed, and no evil would harm him even in the night.

As Gwako disappeared into the dark night, loud prayers were still going on in Mecha's house a few meters downhill from Senta's house. The songs, drums, claps and prayers were more vigorous as they cast the powers of *nyachieni* out of their midst and called upon the Almighty Almighty to take control.

Chapter Three

Vincent Senta was born and raised in Mayenga village. As a youngster, he dutifully teamed up with other village boys to lead goats, sheep and calves to the pastures on the hills. Here, they mounded earth into little pots, toy vehicles, aeroplanes, animals or anything. They built little huts out of twigs and skated on banana grooves downhill. Skating downhill was dangerous, but it was the most exciting adventure as the speed was equated to that of Safari Rally cars. The fastest skater was the hero of the day and won the admiration from peers who cheered him as he cruised with lightning speed. These were enjoyable pastimes for the children. The games could go on with no one remembering when it was time for lunch, until a concerned mother went calling after them. Then, they would all go to one home for lunch, usually of potatoes and banana paste. Once lunch was over, they would head back to the hills to continue with their games. Come evening, the goats, sheep and calves would be nowhere in sight and more often, they had strayed to the neighbouring crop fields, damaged them and eventually, found their ways home. What awaited the boys were backlashes for a job poorly done.

From the tops of the hills, two fierce streams flowed downhill unabated to a fall, *egetogomera*. Fetching water from the streams was difficult due to their incessant speed, and steep positioning. Side by side, lush bushes and hard but smooth rocks bordered the streams. Myths existed that big three-headed snakes lived there roaming and looking for children to lick and eat. And out of curiosity, the brave ones approached the streams cautiously, if only to catch sight of the big three-headed serpents. No child had allegedly been licked or eaten. No peer reported ever seeing one, though myths abound that they came out of the streams to bask and play on the rocks.

The streams were significant as natural boundaries between neighbouring clans, and neighbours loathed interfering with their natural flow, as doing so would amount to disrespecting the boundaries set by ancestors. Further down, the waters provided a natural habitat for lush reeds used to thatch roofs, and ponds in which muddy fish, a protein source, amply flourished. As a child, Senta occasionally and fearfully visited the streams out of curiosity to see the three-headed snakes, but was never lucky enough to catch sight of even a tadpole.

An incident that lingered in his memory for a time and remained ingrained into his adulthood was his visit to one of the streams. He was around eight and very adventurous. His father had bought him a new pair of shorts which doubled as his best for attending church services and as part of his school uniform. One weekend morning, he decided to wash them at one of the streams instead of going downhill to the falls, where women and children washed their clothes. He took a bucket, tied it with a rope and headed to the stream across from their house. He approached the stream very cautiously lest the three-headed reptiles on the rocks beside the river banks, basking, playing and waiting for children to lick and eat, emerged unnoticed, licked and ate him. He looked around and when he could not see any, he stood on a rock at the bank and watched the fast flowing waters race downhill with a rattling sound and a lustrous speed. Then, very cautiously, he lowered his bucket into the stream to fill it with water. Inside it was his pair of shorts! The currents were stronger than him and forcefully "snatched" his bucket leaving him holding the rope. He watched in tears as the bucket and his shorts somersaulted in the bubbly waves downhill until they disappeared in a purplish swivel. With that, he was left with no shorts for school and church service. Now, the myths were confirmed. The reptiles actually lived in the streams and were responsible for his predicament; he had come to a close shave with them.

He left the scene in a hurry with his rope in hand, crying and screaming downhill to the fall where his mother, Nyaboe, and other village women had congregated to fetch water and do their daily chores such as laundering clothes. He explained to his mother, in tears, how he had gone to the stream with the bucket to fetch water and wash his new pair of shorts and how one of the big three-headed serpents had promptly snatched the bucket and his shorts, swallowed and swam with them downhill with the currents. His greatest fear was that he had no shorts and would not be able to attend school and church services.

The women had a prolonged laughter. "We have constantly warned you not to go to the streams lest the snakes lick and eat you," his mother admonished him. "You're lucky they didn't lick and swallow you. By now, I would not have a son called Senta."

Moments later, Nyaboe fetched the bucket from behind a bush. Inside it was his pair of shorts! "The serpent ran with them here, but as adults, we were smarter than it. We snatched them from its jaws before it could eat and swallow them." Nyaboe raised the bucket with one hand and the pair of shorts with the other. "Here it is. Take it, but don't attempt to go near the streams again. Next time you may not be so lucky," she sternly warned him.

Senta's face beamed with excitement but he still remained shaken. At least, he had his new pair of shorts, but he had narrowly survived from the jaws of the serpent. He reflected. He smiled broadly holding his mother's lesso as he ignorantly inquired, "Where is the serpent, mama?"

"It has gone into hiding, son" Nyaboe sympathetically answered, attentively massaging his head. "It ran back uphill upon seeing us. These snakes fear grown-ups but can lick and eat children."

"When I grow up, mama, I shall hunt these serpents and slay them!" he firmly promised as he held onto his mother's skirt.

"You're my kingpin. I shall cook for you, son, to grow healthy and strong, to slay the beasts," Nyaboe supportively assured as she picked him up.

Later, as a grown-up, he came to realize that there were no three-headed or any meaningful snakes at the streams. These were myths coined by the parents to prevent children from going to the fast-flowing streams that could easily pose dangers to them.

Senta grew up as an exceptionally witty, ever inquisitive, though a little adventurous, obedient child. He had agile legs and a sharp brain and memory.

In school, he was brilliant, leading in his class from the lower classes from primary to secondary school. He had empathy and sympathy for his colleagues and took time to assist them with their homework. When the final primary examination results were announced, he had scored the highest marks in the county. With stellar examination results in hand, Senta proceeded to Starehe School where he became a centre of interest amongst peers. He was a footballer, and his long agile legs were great for long races. And when the form four results were announced, Senta emerged among the top in his class. He had scored impressive grades and was admitted to the University of Nairobi to study law.

All those years, he never forgot the absurd incident when he almost lost his treasured pair of shorts to the jaws of the serpents at the village's stream.

Chapter Four

Senta's ambition as he grew up had been to join a Catholic seminary. As a staunch Catholic, he was baptised and given the name Vincent after a local priest. However, when he met Anna at the market one evening and started dating her, he bewitchingly lost focus on becoming a Catholic missionary and lived for her. He cohabited with her immediately after college. Before he knew it, he had unintentionally "broken her legs" in one of the boys' adventures. She had inadvertently conceived. Anna had just sat for her grade twelve examinations and with the turn of events, her desire to proceed further with her education was brought to an end.

Once the news reached the elders in Mayenga, they convened and agreed that Senta's family had offended the family of Chief Mogi. Senta's family had two options in order to "heal the wounds" they had created through their son's activity in order to build cordial ties with Chief Mogi's family. They could either compensate the family of Mogi with two cows for milk for the child to be born, or Senta marries Anna. Upon payment of the cows, Senta was to take charge of the child's expenses.

Though, it appeared a belated imposition, Senta's path with Anna had already been mapped. Anna moved into Senta's home with the baby almost immediately after the baby's birth. That marked the end of her career advancement. He left Anna at home in the care of his parents to proceed with his education at Law school, before they had the first Christian wedding ever to be held in Mayenga.

Standing about six feet tall, with a round face, brilliant sharp eyes, shades of emerging hair, a beard cropped to his chin and an emerging moustache on the upper lip, Vincent Senta easily stood out from the crowd as a handsome man. He was always smartly dressed in tailored suits, matching shirts and neckties.

Vincent Senta's wedding with Anna was the first one of its kind in Mayenga. All along, young men and women met and married in "come we stay" arrangements. Though dowry was later paid, as tradition held, to signify that marriage had occurred thus giving it a legal foundation, the pastors were never involved. So, when Vincent announced that he was marrying Anna in a church, the whole village of Mayenga was engulfed in obvious curiosity as church weddings were rare. Weddings were taken to be special and beyond reach for the ordinary village life. Therefore, the village took it upon itself to make the wedding arrangements in order to witness and to ensure this rare approach to marriage was a success. Chief Mogi, Anna's father, had visited Areba's home with elders from his clan for dowry negotiation. As customs demanded, Areba had paid six cows, a bull and a goat.

Many villagers contributed towards the wedding. There were baskets full of millet and sorghum, bales of pineapples, groundnuts, chapattis and gourds of milk to feed the congregation. As tradition demanded, an occasion like this, food was made available to all. Despite being a Christian wedding, beer was brewed in pots and drums and made available to visitors and villagers.

On the eve of the wedding day, the church was decorated with ribbons of various colours, fresh twigs, climbers and tendrils to signify uniqueness and freshness. Road sides were cleared and swept clean by a combined effort of the villagers. On the day of the wedding, the church was packed to full capacity by young and old with baffled excitement written on their faces. As it was the first wedding of its kind in Mayenga, there was intense curiosity as the congregation watched Anna in spotlessly white wedding dress and veil covering her head, escorted by the bridal party, march to the altar holding her father's hand. Vincent was meticulously dressed in a white double breasted suit as he stood at the altar ready to take his wedding vows and exchange wedding rings. The crowd was baffled when the couple fed each other with a piece of the wedding cake and even more baffled when Anna and Vincent kissed each other as the congregation watched. The affection for each other they were displaying before the crowd was strange in Mayenga as this was an alien culture. However, the occasion was marked with ululations from women and whistles of approval from men. To make the occasion even more memorable, songs were belted and dances performed as the wedding procession of the bride and groom headed out of the church compound to the homestead of Areba soon after the church ceremony:

Mireri mirereri
Mireri mireri
Mirererii
Mireri mirereri
Mireri mireri
Mirereriii

1. *Eraa nyamasonga yasonga Anna korwa sobo*
   Eraa nyamasonga yasonga Anna korwa sobo
2. *Moiseke kare sobo nigo anga eyanga maroboto*
   Moiseke kare sobo nigo anga eyanga maroboto
3. *Momura kare sobo n'etwani nyarogoncho*
   Momura kare sobo n'etwani nyarogoncho
4. *Moiseke kare sobo nigo anga omoswa maritati*

Moiseke kare sobo nigo anga omoswa maritati
5. Momura kare sobo n'erirubi nyabosongo
Momura kare sobo n'erirubi nyamong'ento

Translated as:

Mireri mirereri
Mireri mireri
Mirererii
Mireri mirereri
Mireri mireri
Mirereriii

1. Pursuit of leisure made Anna to move from her home
   Pursuit of leisure made Anna to move from her home
2. A girl in her home is like a second hand cloth
   A girl in her home is like a second hand cloth
3. A man in his home is a crested cock
   A man in his home is a crested cock
4. A girl in her home is a peacock
   A girl in her home is a peacock
5. A man in his home is a poisonous cobra
   A man in his home is a charged cobra

Apart from entertaining the guests, the song had messages: every girl of age attracts a suitor and at some stage needs to move out to her own homestead to start life anew. Once in her house, her beauty may fade with the strains of life; the birth of children, the effort to take care of them and her husband and the demands of society on women. And men, whose roles as breadwinners and protectors of the homes, need to assume these roles like crested cocks or charged cobras.

The wedding ceremony was followed by a honeymoon for the pair to the coast to reflect on the occasion. "You're the pillar of my life," Senta said lovingly, holding Anna close to his chest that weekend after the wedding ceremony.

"Pillar?" Anna asked laughing with a tinge of naivety.

You're the candle that lights my heart."

"Your candle?"

"You're the moon and stars that shine on my path," he emphasised lovingly.

"Moon?"

"You're the pearl and love of my life."

"Love. Yes! Love is in my dreams. It's what I was waiting to hear and what every one of us dreams about. Love and children - to make us whole. I love you my sweet," Anna implored kissing him hard on his cheek.

"You're all that I have said. Which colour of dress would you prefer this time my charming pillar?" Senta asked as they enjoyed their honeymoon in the Beach Hotel, as the Indian Ocean waves rolled back onto themselves, delightfully sending bluish misty sprays into the atmosphere.

"Sky blue, like the waves of the ocean, arrests my eyes, my husband," she radiantly replied revealing a set of whitish teeth. "It reflects the clarity of the sky when it is cloudless. Then in the evenings, I prefer red. In it, I fathom a loving night close to my husband," she said chuckling in a hearty laughter and in imagination.

"And for our compound?" Senta probed gently.

"Green is the colour I like for our compound," she soothingly answered. "Green holds the secrets of life. A green country means the ability to produce food and feed its people and multiply. Consider it; a silent weekend afternoon in this background, and a loving family beside me. I'll wish to live forever," Anna fantasized popping her eyes slyly onto the sky.

"You're right, my love," Vincent said. "Green is the colour of the universe. It means life. Plants and animals that ensure foods are on the table. I would love to live in a green countryside. And that is why I'd love we set our home in there; away from the stressful city with bustling noises and polluted air."

"You like food too much," Anna teased. "Yet, you don't gain flesh on your body."

Vincent laughed. "This is how I like my body to be. Lean! To beat the emergent dietary diseases: diabetes, cancer, pressure and even premature aging. Then I'll live the bonuses of my years."

In this blissful conversation, they decided to set up their home in the village of Mayenga. This would allow Vincent to have closer contact with his roots in the village that he loved so much. "I hope you won't be too lonely when I'm in Nairobi."

"You need to eat my chapattis over the weekends," Anna joked amiably.

"Every weekend, of course," Vincent promised firmly, smiling heartily.

"Our people of Mayenga," Vincent reminisced thoughtfully, "are a great people. They require encouragement and somebody to show them the way to development. Through that, they will see the light, live in the current reality and improve their quality of life."

"I remember how they sang heartily at our wedding," Anna interjected thoughtfully, demonstrating how they danced. "I saw the enthusiasm of a people who are going somewhere but have lost their path. They miss the fullness of life, but they don't have a way out."

"They need to retrace their way through reengineering. It's us who are better exposed who can make a difference in them. Pillar, you have seen the waters flowing from the top of the hill to the falls without any tapping. We go all the way downhill to fetch it and load it on our heads, then head all the way back uphill," Vincent sadly observed. "Even a donkey doesn't need to do that much work. I hate to see my mother in her frail energy trudging downhill and uphill with that heavy load. Yet, water is life!"

"I hail the women and children who do it. But then, is it necessary?" Anna asked desolately.

"It isn't," he answered. "Something needs to be done."

"But who can do it?" Anna asked resignedly. "Who can see sense in Mayenga?"

"It can start with us." He stood up from his chair and paced thoughtfully around the room. "One can't live peacefully in a community that utterly lacks the basic necessities of life. And one can't run away from his people to maintain a settled conscience elsewhere," he reasoned loudly. "That water flowing downhill can be tapped for use and this can change the way of life in the village." He turned and looked at Anna. "Pillar," he called his wife. "If some of the water can be stopped and tapped at the source, the unnecessary suffering of the women going downhill to fetch it and load it uphill can be ameliorated," Vincent noted beaming.

"I concur entirely," Anna said cheerfully. "That's a great idea. But dear, who will do it? Who sees the need? Our men can't as they don't feel the load," she reasoned. "They will shoot down the idea, even before it hatches," she mused.

"It can start with us. I've an idea. We can mobilize the women of Mayenga as a start, and sell the idea to them. Women here feel the pinch and are amenable to innovations. I'm sure they will laud the idea. Then, we can very humanely ask the men to come in and lend their contribution," he reasoned. "I'm sure they will see the need. If they don't, we shall proceed with the women and slay the mythical three-headed reptiles living there. After all, it requires one person's idea to change the world, a few people's idea to make a greater change, and the masses to destroy it. I'm willing to fire the first shot."

"That can be a great start," Anna concurred with a warm smile. "It will give them a sense of worth, and improve the quality of their lives. Though I'm comfortable with rain-harvested water in the tank in our house, I hate to see mum going downhill for water. I'll lend my hand in the endeavour."

Senta decided to revisit their counselling session with the pastor before their wedding. "Families are unique, and can have their own unique problems," he noted. "Each family, including ours, will have its intricate problems, but each has a way of dealing with its issues. In the end, an amicable solution should be found," he diligently observed. "I agree we endeavour to tackle our issues together without any external parties. I see it as the best way."

"Dear, I liked the way the pastor dwelled on the family life. It was gentle and elaborate. Ours is not different from others. I anticipate that our problems, if and when they arise, should be our challenges, and we should learn to solve them amicably between us and without any external forces." Anna attentively agreed.

Chapter Five

Mayenga was a sleepy, disillusioned, veiled hill, though from the outlook, it was an ordinary rural village. Access to Mayenga was difficult as all roads leading there had never been developed. The preferable means of transport was by foot, through steep minders. It was concealed from reality, though life went on as usual. It was largely unfelt except during the general elections when politicians thronged there to entice people and buy their votes. Politicians hardly sold their ideologies as people never listened to them. Even if they did, the eligible voters had wanting needs that demanded immediate solutions. Ignorantly, they thought, these were the right times to satisfy their "stomachs" and receive hand-outs. They voted for those who had oil to grease their palms. So, politicians made their frantic last minute competition with goodies and cash to win their hearts, but disappeared immediately after the elections, only to reappear during the next one.

Getting an audience from the people of Mayenga was a hard nut to crack. If one proposed holding a rally, one needed cash hand-outs for attendees. If hand-outs were not forthcoming, then future rallies of a kind would have no audience. People came out to listen to rallies with the expectation of receiving hand-outs. They believed in themselves, and new ideas that did not fill their immediate needs were seen with pessimism and were shot down at the first opportunity or never received support. Their culture was the norm, although a wind of change was blowing from everywhere, driven by the prevailing economy, information flow and interactions. Cheap liquor, petty gossip and idling in the market centre were the order of the day, especially for the men. The role of putting food on the table was largely left to women. Children, especially girls, were hard hit as they were the constant source of family labour. They hardly stayed in school to complete their studies. More so, they were seen as a source of wealth for their male siblings and fathers once they got married. And many girls unwittingly opted for early marriages instead of education at a time when they were least prepared to confront the challenges of life. Illicit sex was the norm. Many girls had kids out of wedlock and unwittingly exposed themselves to the potential ravages of attendant diseases including HIV/AIDS. The usual thing was to blame evil eyes, witches, and spirits of displeased ancestors yearning to be appeased through sacrifices. The boy child was not spared either. With no positive role models to emulate, many dropped out of school and took to drinking illicit beer as the preferred pastime. Life was hard for everybody, more so for the women who bore the brunt of the hardships, trying to survive a day at a time. It was a bitter cry, especially from women who had little chance of breaking from the vicious circle of deprivation.

Though, it rained frequently, water, more so clean drinking water, was a problem. The two streams with their source on the hill snaked their way downhill without any tapping, to the falls, *egetogomera*, where women and girls congregated in the evenings to draw water for their families' daily needs. Then, they would carry their loads uphill to their respective homes. Though tedious, for ages, no one saw the need of tapping water uphill to save the time and effort now expended in meeting household water needs. The houses were all mud-walled with thatches of Rhodes grass available on the hillsides, and water reeds from the valleys.

Vincent Senta had established himself as an "eye of Mayenga" when he single-handedly opened up a neglected road from the market to his home in the village. The idea was to access his home with ease by car, but it ended up earning him a name as it provided a better access to Mayenga. His temperate approach to issues and ideas had warmed and won him many hearts in Mayenga. Having had a better education and exposure than everybody else in the village, he was viewed differently and with awe by many. As their son, and having grown up within the village, he understood well the thinking of the village. He empathized with the level of abject poverty and the harsh conditions the villagers unknowingly lived in. He had a resolve to make a change in the lives of the people of Mayenga. He had ideas in every sector, and openly shared with the people whenever an opportunity arose. He wanted more and quality education for the youngsters; quality of life and dignity devoid of stress. They listened to him, and some were positive towards his ideas and approaches. Some were sceptical, arguing that he was seeking power, he had a job and didn't understand the lowly life of Mayenga, and that he had a lot of money to dish out. Wasn't he merely interested in becoming a member of parliament or a governor? They concluded that he was only using them as a stepping stone for his own advancement and personal gain.

The level of poverty in Mayenga, compounded with unemployment of both human and tangible resources, was abhorrent. The youth whiled away productive time in unproductive undertakings. Peddling cheap liquor and drugs were considered a good and normal pastime, despite the toll they were taking on the young men. Men and youth fought for dignity in brawls and hauls of vulgarity, not realising that dignity is earned through integrity and hard work. The elders jostled in "separating and uniting" them in never ending brawls over trivialities in time consuming and impromptu *barazas* to earn a living with little success. It was a pathetic situation.

Mayenga was a village unknowingly troubled with beliefs of witchcraft and negative perceptions. The intention was in the essence of life. Indeed they had their children go to school, but they did not go far because they never believed in education as a serious undertaking. Their conscience told them that an educated person could not find life in a village stifled with witchcraft and evil eyes. Unfortunately, few people believed that education in itself held meaning to life. They never thought about "tomorrow," believing that "tomorrow would sort itself out," and therefore they lived each day at a time. They went around and around looking for solutions from witch doctors and diviners, attributing every misfortune to acts of witchcraft, evil eyes and supernatural spirits out loose to torment them.

Cultivation of the land was done as a way of life, producing little harvest despite the potential of the land to yield more. Though they were advised in *barazas* that if they added value to those small pieces of land they had, they could harvest better yields, they attributed poor harvests to acts of wicked eyes, and roaming spirits in the fields, destroying crops and creating unfavourable weather patterns. In the planting seasons, many villagers would secretly visit diviners and witch doctors in search of blessings for improved crop yields. This was not done for free. They spent a lot of money and time in these ventures to have their seeds and fields blessed.

Once they planted, some did not bother to weed the germinated seeds, as the diviners and witch doctors had already assured them of a good harvest. And when the yields were poor, the diviner could be dismissed as impotent and another one consulted, or another omen was used as an excuse for the cause. Pessimism about the future was very rife. "Eat what you can lay your hands on, for tomorrow, we do not know how it will break," they villagers believed. So, saving for a rainy day was non-existence. Granaries were usually empty of food shortly after a harvest season.

Men were often seen drunk and expecting hand-outs from whoever appeared to be better off than them. They lived their lives in beer dens, drinking and making merry. Alcohol was cheap and was the valued business of choice for many homes, with its effect wrecking men and youth to desolate states. Their merry making, thwarted their effort to raise school fees for their children. They considered fees a big cost that could deny them their leisure. Women were used as tools, and could not ask questions as their husbands' words were divine and final. They woke up early to till the land, fetch water and firewood, and place food on the table for their men and children. After initiation, boys took the paths of their fathers. It was bitter crying, sighing and murmuring episodes, but women could not ask questions or complain openly lest they were labelled rebels, headstrong, unmarriageable and consequently banished to their matrimonial homes together with their children to "learn" from their mothers how to respect their husbands. Life was a struggle, without one with a convincing tongue to deliver them out of this turmoil.

The government often took blame for the problems. It had failed to provide employment and facilities for the people. And the people vented their desperation. The government's presence was hardly felt except during the frequent raids of beer dens by the administration police (AP), where those rounded up and arrested were forced to part with cash for the officers to secure their release.

Most of the time, Senta found himself asking questions. "Was I born in a strange and forgotten land? What could be the way out of this turmoil? How would Mayenga live in the current times and compete in a global society? How would it get out of this mess?" But it dawned on him that the cries and tears that were unknowingly shed for a long time were going to be wiped by a cloth of knowledge.

Senta's ambitions were invigorated by his peers to change the village for the better. Having been educated and having worked in the city, he had experienced life outside the village. He visited Mayenga regularly accompanied by his friends to see his family and for church functions. He realized that to change the village that sturdily believed in traditional culture and witchcraft, the church needed to play a greater role. Among those in his regular entourage was a son of renowned city pastor. After a tour through the village, the friends could see the suffering of women and children. They did not like the age-old idea of women fetching water from downstream when the same water could be tapped upstream or rain-harvested. They added fire to his water project idea, that through the church and women's groups, he could reach the people and make an impression on their attitudes. They offered to donate towards the water project if only to change the pathetic situation of Mayenga.

Senta dedicated his resources and time to the project, which required patience and personal sacrifice. He had to employ a good tongue to win the trust and confidence of the people of Mayenga, and then create a platform to change their attitudes and perceptions. A "good tongue," they say, "brings cows home from afar." It convinces a snake to come out of its hiding and makes a mean person bring food and share it with others. To succeed one needs to accompany these attributes with good oration, and fortunately, he was gifted in the art of communication.

So, Vincent assembled a group of women of Mayenga one afternoon and floated the idea of pulling together to tap the water upstream from the two streams flowing downhill. Women were easier to handle in this respect as the objective would lighten their problems. They instantly praised the idea and were willing to lend all they could to accomplish the mission. "It pains us to carry containers downhill, loading them, and then carry the loads uphill to our homes," they said in unison. "Water is our need. It's life!"

Immediately, the idea was put in motion. They set up a committee to oversee the project and agreed to contribute little by little to buy water pipes, other accessories and provide their labour towards the project. It was immediately called Mayenga Women's Group Water Project, later Mayenga Water Project or simply Water Project.

Vincent consulted with a few village elders, who assisted him to reach the men and convince them of the value of this idea. It was a splendid idea that could work to change the lives of the people of Mayenga for the better, he argued. It would transform the lives of women and girls by affording them more time to do other duties while improving the quality of lives in the village. However, there had to be hand gifts for the elders if Vincent wanted their participation and a chance to make them see the need for change in

Mayenga and realize his mission. For that, Senta parted with a handsome sum of money for the village elders to support the project. Their jobs were to mobilize and sensitize the village on the Water Project idea and convince them to attend Water Project related meetings that were aimed at seeking support for the Water Project.

Many elders saw it differently. Some were happy that a source had turned out to grease their palms and they were eager to sensitize and mobilize people, knowing that they would receive hand-outs. The idea was for the village to see life with their heart and not their eyes. To have a desire different from the situation they were engulfed in, and that the project was for their own good.

Indeed the idea of mobilising villagers worked, and many villagers attended Senta's briefing meetings. He sold his ideas never knowing that people would accept them. There was uncertainty whether they could let the waters from the streams be "tampered" with. He told them about education and realized that people wanted to know more about their lives. In the meetings, he brought more guest speakers who could address the issues pertaining to lives of the people in Mayenga. Some came to listen but never bought the ideas and went on with their lives as usual, while others were enthusiastic. Women especially, took the ideas with fervent passion, and Senta was happy that he was being rewarded to change Mayenga village for the better. As one of their own, there was no way they could deny him and that was a kick-start.

To win the confidence of the villagers further, he had to set an example to emulate. He had set one by constructing a modest house for himself and his parents against the backdrop of pessimism. The general feel was that a modest house would attract the wrath of evil eyes and with that one could not be assured of peace or longevity. Now he had to work hard to oversee the Mayenga Water Project. He and his friends donated handsomely for the initial work on the project. The women's meagre contributions gradually boosted the Water Project's kitty.

When the government heard of a unique Water Project, it made its presence in Mayenga in terms of expertise and coordination. Millie, the county water coordinator, whose attempts to make in-roads to the village but had often been thwarted by suspicion, saw it as a God-sent opportunity to make her presence felt. Senta became handy in helping her realize her dreams. She aggressively teamed up with him, and with synergy, the pair advanced their common cause.

From the contributions in the kitty, the women bought pipes and water tanks, dug the trenches, laid the pipes with the assistance of the county water coordinator and finally tapped the waters upstream. This lightened their load of fetching water from downhill. It provided clean drinking water, and the aggressive ones started to water their gardens from the water taps with more ease. Some created watering holes for their animals around the taps in their homes. This left them with more time to spare for other activities.

The atmosphere was ecstatic when Vincent Senta arrived in Mayenga in a convoy of vehicles accompanied by his wife, Anna, his friends and Millie, to commission the Water Project whose fame had resoundingly spread in the entire region. Mayenga Women's Group was singing and dancing in the field in praise of the Water Project.

Ee obuya obuya
Obuya bokare Mayenga
Obuya obuya
Obuya bokare Mayenga
Tema naende
Tema naende Mayenga
Tema naende
Tema naende Mayenga

Bwabokire
Bwabokire obwanchani
Bwabokire
Bwabokire obwanchani
Boria bwakare
Boria bwakare obwanchani

Translates as:

Ee the goodies
The goodies at Mayenga
The goodies
The goodies at Mayenga

Try again
Try again at Mayenga
Try again
Try again at Mayenga

Love has been revitalized
Love has been revitalized at Mayenga
Love has been revitalized
Love has been revitalized at Mayenga
The old love
The old love of Mayenga

Senta's team enthusiastically joined in the song and dance. They jigged for awhile before taking seats at the dais. After the people had settled, Senta took to the podium. In a booming voice and matching eloquence, he addressed the audience amidst cheers. "Our people, people of Mayenga, I salute you. As one of your sons, my heart is in Mayenga. I desire to see you have a quality life, and that was the essence of the Water Project. I would love to see Mayenga moving forward in tandem with the emerging trends, and that way life would have a lot of meaning. What had made sense in the days of our predecessors may not do it now. If we fail to live to the challenges, we shall find ourselves on the wrong side of the coin. I say so because I'm one of you, among the equal," he said amidst cheers.

"The Water Project was an uphill battle when we started. I grew up here seeing the streams flowing downhill to the falls, and as a child, I fetched water and carried it uphill to the homestead. It was tedious! I was led to believe that there were three-headed snakes which inhabited the streams, coming out by day to bask on the rocks and looking for children who went there, in order to lick and eat. With the Water Project, today we have slain the beasts," he said confidently surveying the crowd who acknowledged his speech with more cheers. "Clean drinking water is really important for Mayenga. Why should the streams flow downhill for ages and why not tap them uphill?"

"When we consulted our friends and shared with them our trepidation, they encouraged us. Millie came in handy. She is a great officer with her heart in Mayenga. When challenges appeared to overwhelm us, they told us, 'When you are doing something, you should try to finish it. If indeed the project is just foolish, then quit and don't waste your time. Time is valuable.' They gave us a hand in terms of resources and expertise. My friend here," pointing to the son of a pastor, "was with us in prayers. We persisted, and through it the doors were opened. We're here because you persisted."

There was clapping and loud cheers of appreciation from the crowd. They saw Senta as one who had their interest at heart and as their hero.

"People of Mayenga," Senta proceeded. "I don't need to convince you that education opens doors. Trust me if you will. Trust is something that I strongly believe in and take seriously. It is the thing that holds our society together. Without trust, life would be meaningless. It holds families together, maintains friendship, and keeps society moving forward in a civilised way. I was advantaged enough to have been exposed to education," he said. "We need to re-examine our beliefs and attitudes, and embrace change to move forward," he stated. "What's it that is holding Mayenga back from realising her dreams? The answers are with us. No one really cares about Mayenga. It doesn't bother them if the youth go to school or whether there is food or water in the homes. Let's empower our youth through education and appropriate training. Let them not whittle away with unproductive dreams. Let's remove illiteracy and ignorance through education. Our roads are impassable and our people are dying of treatable diseases. We can pick up the pieces, retrace our footsteps and move forward. We need to tap and harness our human resources because this is our heritage. Let's kick poverty out of our homes with hard work. Our time should be spent productively. And finally, let's put those aspects of culture that have held us back, behind us. Negative culture breeds hatred, poverty and impacts negatively on the quality of our lives. If it is our beliefs holdings us back, we can discard them and move with the times as culture is a factor of time. Our problems are within reach and have solutions," he articulated.

"Today I commission the Mayenga Water Project. It is dedicated to the women who painstakingly mobilized and organised themselves into a viable women's group. They contributed in kind towards the project, and laboured to dig trenches. The water tanks will harvest and store clean drinking water. It's our challenge that our youth and our men would emulate them by keeping grade cows and water them from the tanks. Grade cows will supply enough milk for Mayenga, and the excess, we shall sell to raise fees for our children and meet our essential needs."

"He is doing this because he has an eye for parliament," one drunken man shouted. "Let him finish and grease our palms."

"Mmm," a section of men booed him. "What he is telling us is what we need. This is the eye of Mayenga. He has no seat, yet he spends time to see to our welfare."

"You are too much of a drunk," another man rebuked him menacingly.

Chapter Six

The Water Project was a milestone event in the village of Mayenga. People began to see and appreciate that they could change their lives for the better through their own involvement. The laborious work of going downhill to the falls, *egetogomera*, to fetch water and then carry it uphill became a thing of the past. Women and children met at the taps to fetch water and do their laundry, singing in praise of the water. Water-borne diseases that were a menace and disillusioned the village, frequently sending people to seek treatment, were reduced to almost zero. To access the project, a road had been upgraded to reach the site and electricity supplied to run water dowsing pumps. All these made life in Mayenga bearable. The village innovators took advantage of the water and electricity to come up with income generating projects. Kundi dug a trench directing waste runoff to his Napier farm. He went further and laid pipes to tap the water to his house. Two people were employed to man the project: a watchman, to guard the site, and a pump attendant to treat the water with water treatment chemicals supplies from the county water office, and operate the water dowsing pumps. The project became a case study in the region and many people thronged there to see, learn from it and implement the idea at their villages.

The water project was run by the village. They elected a management team to ensure its smooth running. The team met and set rules on how best to run it. Each household was required to pay a paltry ten shillings per month to meet the salaries of the watchman and pump attendant. The remaining sum was to be used to meet the cost of repairs and replacement of worn-out parts and systems. The county had pledged to supply water treatment chemicals, the expertise needed for any works, and oversee the success of the project. A fine was further imposed on anyone who came to the site under intoxication, used abusive language or fought at the site. Those who wilfully caused damage to the system and those who had refused to support the Water Project were to be denied access to the water or asked to pay a fine before they could be allowed to use it. The rules were ardently lauded by the village.

A week after the project was commissioned, Nyamwanda, the skins and hides dealer, who had termed the project as "composed of village idiots digging a mole hole," came to the laundry with his dirty skins and hides to wash them, but the watchman denied him access as he had refused to be part of the project. He had not contributed a penny or provided labour to it despite being requested several times to do so. In retaliation, he flashed a machete and threatened to slash the watchman and anyone who interfered with his life. He forced his way in and washed his raw skins and dirty hides. The committee convened and summoned him to appear before it, but he refused to attend, deeming them a bunch of village idiots. Earlier, they had supported him as one of their own, to be elected a chairman of the skins and hides dealers in the county. He had bribed the youth with illicit liquor to intimidate his opponents to surrender to him. He was used to bulldozing his way. Those who tried to venture into his trade at the market were miserably frustrated or hurt as it was rumoured that he could hire a bunch of thugs or even employ witchcraft to vanquish the opponents. His morbid jealousy attracted as much hate as fear. But the villagers continued to supply him with their skins and hides at an insignificant price, which he sold at huge profits, something they did because they had no other alternative.

Mecha's wife Moraa also came to fetch water from the taps. She explained to the watchman that it was Mecha himself who had asked her to go for the water. Mecha was in a hurry to attend an Almighty Almighty function, and she was obligated to prepare a meal for him. She was asked to pay a fine of ten shillings which she failed to raise. It took the intervention of Senta to have her allowed to use the water on condition that she and Mecha would support future projects.

Morwabe, the village rumour monger, never supported the idea from its inception. He did not contribute a penny or labour, and true to his words, he did not drink its water. He spent most of his time at the market place where he acted as if he knew everything, even where and how the sun slept and when it would wake up. He had answers and excuses to every situation and could talk endlessly to anybody who bothered to listen to him. More often, he was pessimistic about everything. At the end of his lengthy indolence, as a rule, he would beg for some coins to buy a cup of tea to replenish his lost energy. Few people bothered to acknowledge his request. As a result, he was emaciated.

He had had heartless words for the project. "The Water Project is a hoax to mint money for some individuals," he had discredited it unreservedly. "Show me a single project that has ever succeeded in Mayenga? All the projects we're told about, the leaders end up pocketing the proceeds and growing their tummies. Let the streams God created flow downhill undisturbed, as our ancestors found and left them.

Our women have not complained that fetching water from the falls is tedious or bad," he had hotly argued.

However, when the project succeeded and the taps started to flow, he changed his tone. "Actually," he argued. "The project is not Senta's brain-child. It's of no good to Mayenga. It's a government project, and Senta is only being used to advance the government's cause by convincing the women to adopt it. The daily chemical dosages meant to treat the water as they cheat us, aren't meant to kill germs and control water-borne diseases, but to enforce family planning to the village," he quipped in the market. "Our people will be infertile shells with time, and Mayenga will have no descendants. Then the aged ones will slowly die of cancer," he added. "I drink water direct from the streams and when it rains, I harvest it from my grass-thatched roof. It's safe as I have not been sick," he emphasised, evoking fear into the minds. "Have you ever asked yourselves why that woman, Millie, who dresses like a man, is ever present in Mayenga? Or why Senta has refused to increase his household, when we all know he has a lot of money to give to Mayenga?" He could ask and answer himself, "who knows? Perhaps he could have drunk lots of these waters and Millie could be out on an undisclosed mission. Don't you ever see Millie carrying her own water in a bottle? That tells you something!" Why can't she drink water from the taps if it's safe as they cheat us? I hear she buys her water. If she is that genuine, she should give me that money she spends on water to buy myself a cup of tea. However, when asked to clarify, he could not sufficiently convince his listeners why Senta, who appeared to have good intentions for the people, could allow himself to be used against them. His answer was often simple, "why did the devil go against God when he was his archangel?

Chapter Seven

Kundi took the idea of a dairy project being introduced to the village with a lot of keen interest. Two months later, he acquired a grade cow. It cost him all the proceeds of maize and beans for that season, but the returns he anticipated were to be ploughed back in just one crop. He could water it from the water taps with ease. For the first time in Mayenga, a cow was now reared in a zero grazing unit. That was a huge leap.

"This is the best cow you can rear in the village for huge economic gains. The weather is favourably cool and amenable to its healthy stay," the agricultural officer (A.O.) advised him. "A Holstein breed from Holland can produce up to forty litres of milk a day and a calf every year. That is twenty litres in the mornings and twenty in the evenings. Translate that to cash and you are the richest man in the village."

"I have enough Napier grass and Lucerne for the cow," Kundi informed him joyfully. "With the water from the project, my Napier and Lucerne won't be hard hit with dry spells. And for the supplements, I'll get them from Kisii town."

"The major problem here is ECF (East Coast Fever), brought about by ticks. To ensure the cow is safe, spray it with Tri-ticks once a week," the officer advised. "Keep records of it for easy management and get in touch with us whenever a need arises."

When the agricultural officer left, Kundi was left counting how lucky he was. A cow that would pull him out of poverty once it calved. He wasn't going to be the same again, and he would meet his financial needs with ease. He became busier than before. He was up and down fetching Napier grass and water from the water project tanks for the cow, chaffing Napier to chewable sizes and feeding it like a baby. He sprayed it with Tri-ticks once a week using an improvised pump. However, he had one fear: the witches of Mayenga! Would they leave his cow untouched? No one had ever kept a grade cow in the village or prospered and was left untouched. It was believed that any progressive project that one started stalled halfway through due to what was attributed to witches who did not want to see one succeed or make progress.

Word quickly went around that Kundi had acquired a breeding cow; a cow that did not roam in the fields with other cows, but lived in a house like a human being. There was fervent curiosity, and many villagers thronged into his home to see for themselves the new breed. For the first time in many years Mecha visited his home to see the cow, but he kept a safe distance from the animal as his faith could not allow him to go near it. It was a big black cow dotted with white stripes. The udders were sizeable, a sign that it would produce lots of milk once it calved. It was a lovely cow with a full stomach; very kind with alert eyes, always chewing in its pen, and respectfully responding to people's praises.

"It can produce forty litres of milk a day," Kundi jovially informed his visitors.

"With that, you are out of the blacks," Morwabe commented. "You won't have a problem buying me tea at the market," he joked courteously.

Senta was one of the visitors who donated a spray pump to Kundi when he heard that Kundi had taken his advice and acquired a grade cow. He was thrilled when he learnt that Kundi had sold his maize and beans and bought a Friesian. Kundi was more than overjoyed when he received the pump, because he had been spraying his cow using improvised fresh twigs. He immediately named the cow Senta.

"I'll call it Senta because you have provided a pump for it." Then, cow Senta was six months in-calf. It mulched the Napier and licked the salt lick in its shade unlike other cows. It stared at people with keen, kind and soft eyes as if it was listening to their conversations.

When cow Senta was calving, Kundi stayed with her. He brought a mattress and slept in the pen. Two days later, the cow had not calved, nor was she on-feed. The excruciating pain in her stomach caused her to groan from her belly making Kundi very anxious. The calf's forelegs had emerged but its head was not visible. Cow Senta was so tired that she had stopped pushing. "Cow Senta is in trouble. Come and assist us." With urgency, Kundi pleaded with Mecha who was cultivating nearby and stopping momentarily to chase birds from his farm. "Please, we need more hands to deliver the calf."

"I don't touch cows, you know that. Not even their products," Mecha answered firmly and continued with his work. "My faith is unto the Almighty Almighty and the things of this world don't concern me. All animals have gone astray and sinned against the Almighty Almighty, and their blood is too defiled with the sins of this world."

In disgust, Kundi frowned and walked away. Luckily, he met two young men passing by, and together with other villagers, they tried to assist cow Senta. When it became difficult to calf, one man ran to fetch the agricultural officer. Two hours later, the agricultural officer arrived with a veterinarian. By then, Cow Senta was too tired and lay prostrate on the ground, foaming from its mouth, groaning from its belly with tears welling from its once lovely and kind eyes. It died shortly after, as the veterinarian was performing a caesarean section to deliver the calf.

"It died of prolonged labour," the doctor sadly informed them. "The bladder and spleen are fatally punctured," he explained after a post-mortem examination. "The calf was too big for normal parturition. Had you called me in time, perhaps your cow would still be alive and well," he noted sympathetically. "Brother, take heart. As long as you're alive, you will have other cows."

The village was left stunned with the death of cow Senta. "Grade cows don't survive in a village that has a lot of witches," one villager commented. "A calf can't just grow beyond its delivery size. Witches are the reason that none prospers here," it was alleged.

"This is the work of evil eyes. He should have bought something else with the money or even used it for his leisure," Morwabe commented in disgust.

Cow Senta was slaughtered and skinned by Nyamwanda who had rushed to the scene upon hearing that the cow had died. The carcass was shared freely among the villagers as it had not died of a disease. Nyamwanda took its skin, which according to the villagers was the largest and loveliest skin they had ever seen, but what Nyamwanda paid for it was mere peanuts.

Kundi was left mourning and counting the losses. Had Mecha given a helping hand, perhaps his cow could have survived. "How could he blatantly refuse to assist a calving cow just because he doesn't eat meat or drink milk? Yet, he had come to see it when everybody heard that I had acquired a grade cow. Mecha must have bewitched my cow," he concluded bitterly. Like an arrow that killed a kinsman and is hidden in a vent, Kundi always recalled and blamed Mecha for the death of his cow.

Chapter Eight

Anna was in the kitchen washing utensils when Grace popped in through the living room looking perturbed.

"Anna, aah," Grace caught Anna's attention.

"Yes, my dear." Anna looked up concerned.

"This is strange," she said, shaking her head in denial. "Strange, this one." she almost murmured.

"Strange! What's strange, my dear?" Anna inquired in amazement. "Has something bad happened in Mayenga?"

"It's strange indeed. I can't understand how you people think," Grace repeated almost to herself. She appeared thoughtful for a while. "You mean your husband was here two weeks ago and you are seated doing nothing. Then when he comes back, he just pops in and leaves the house as if it's infested with lice?" Grace folded her hands on her chest. "This is unlike him. Ask me and I'll tell you." Grace was firm and unmoving. "A man is a man, they say. They are all the same. Two weeks is a long period for a husband to be away from one's eyes. He comes home and doesn't even stick in the house." Grace moved closer to Anna and gently held her shoulder. "Anna my dear, sometimes I wonder why this must happen to you. Premonitions are important tools to ensure one's path is clear and safe."

"Why do you say so? I don't understand what you are driving at," Anna said politely.

"Indeed you don't. You're my best friend in Mayenga and I can't just watch things go wrong on your side.

Your husband hasn't spent a weekend away from the village since you married," Grace emphasised. "He used to spend all his time with you in this house chatting and laughing. Today, the scenario is different. He is all over the village with women, singing, dancing and cheering him." Grace gyrated sarcastically with her hands holding her loins as if to emulate the acts of the dancing women she imagined. "How secure are you that one of them wouldn't snatch him. Women too have their desires and ways of getting what they want. Further, you believe he is all alone in Nairobi?" Grace stared at Anna quizzically for a moment. "With all these city women thirsty for money and men to provide and keep them company in the harsh reality of life today? He has money and he dishes it out easily to the village idiots. And you know the powers of money. Aah, Anna you are simply fooling yourself," she clapped her hands, posed and paced uneasily as Anna watched her. "My friend you're simply plugging your ears. Then you say he gives you lots of money and presents?" She moved closer to Anna and almost in a whisper said firmly, "No Anna! Of what use are presents if you've no grip on your man? You are lost. I used to envy you, but now, not anymore." Grace shook her head repeatedly in denial. "Now, not anymore," she repeated staring at Anna directly in her eyes. "Now look here my dear. He doesn't use all his money on you alone. Remember he is a public figure with trails of admirers. You must think! I say this because you are my friend."

"Grace, you're my friend," Anna replied. "What do you think is happening to him?" Anna was meditative. "He is an honest and upright man. He is passionate about his family. I trust him and he has always reciprocated this. He is busy with a noble cause for Mayenga. I haven't seen one person who thinks so passionately about a people. Though of late, he is rarely in the house and is more preoccupied with the projects of Mayenga. I have no reason to doubt him. Though, the last time he was here, two weeks ago, he appeared distant. He didn't want to talk much. He didn't have the smiles, the energy or the money he won me with. As he left, he said he was attending a seminar over the weekend. True, he called me from the seminar, but we hear stories that seminars can turn out to be something else."

"You are my best friend. I consider you as my kin sister. I don't want you to suffer and later wonder why I never warned you," Grace emphasised. "Anna, my sister, you are the best friend I have in Mayenga. Now listen, and listen carefully. Men have their crude ways of being cheeky behind the scenes. Nowadays, one can even keep a secret family that a wife will never know of. It only emerges at his funeral. Haven't you heard? Always have an intuition to protect you from trails of eventualities. To be safe, you must keep track of him, Anna. Mine gives me everything. You know Mayaka, and how he was dingy with his money." She stood up and acted tough swinging her bossom, "I, Grace, control his pay slip. Every penny of his! If he wants a drink, I buy it for him myself and bring it into the house."

"Strange," Anna remarked.

"Strange!" Grace walked back to Anna. "What is strange about that? Do you know what I went through to gain control of him?"

"Give him some room to mingle with other men. Life is not all about money. It is about recreation too. It is about others," Anna reasoned.

"It isn't strange. Or am I unreasonable, my friend? I gave him enough room and he mingled enough! I gave him the freedom, but come month-end he would come home with nothing in his pockets. I would turn his pockets inside out while he slept, but I would be met with receipt after receipt of beer, meals and even lodgings," Grace recounted shaking her head. "And when I asked, I was met with silent stares or kicks. Life was hard then, until I became wiser. Now I, Grace, plan for the money."

Anna recalled how Mayaka used to sing and howl on his way home every night. He was known to be the most irresponsible idiot in Mayenga. His hair was kinky, rumpled and he wore a single pair of torn shoes. His clothes were always dirty and patched. More often, he would rain havoc to his entire family, sending them to seek refuge in the neighbourhood homes for the entire night. Today, it is a different story! Indeed, Mayaka had drastically transformed to become a responsible person who was now sober and well-groomed.

"Grace! Aah! I remember what you went through. Now I agree; he is the best man in the village. How did you manage to tame him?" Anna inquired keenly.

Grace moved closer to Anna, took a seat and gently held her back. "Anna, my dear, it is a long story. Being told isn't seeing. And seeing isn't believing until you are there." She fidgeted in her chair and recounted. "Mayaka was the idiot of idiots until he was baptised with fire. I travelled far and wide. Today, I am glad I did. The trick worked, and now he sings to my hymn. If I'm not home in time, he cleans the house, enters the kitchen, washes utensils, lights the fire and cooks; something he would have never dreamed of doing."

"Tell me more," Anna urged on.

"I said I travelled," Grace answered. "I had to move out with other women. Period!"

"I don't understand you. You seem to talk in parables. Trust me with your secrets Grace, if you really value my life," Anna urged, assuring her.

"To be precise, a "doctor" assisted me. She gave me a concoction which I mixed in his food, the meal he loves best. He ate and requested for more. I served him more and he urged that I prepare such meals for him daily. I promised to prepare them in the evenings on condition he was home by then. He promised to be at home for the food. I enumerated the costs of the food, and I made him realize that we couldn't afford it because of the way he spent his money. He agreed to let me manage his pay slip. The following month, he placed all his earnings on the table in front of me. He hasn't let me down since. But he doesn't know that I had to travel to achieve this." She finished her sentence with a glow on her face. "I could be too miserable, Anna, had I not travelled. Now we have enviable communication. We talk past the middle of the night planning our lives."

Anna did not know this side of Grace. Grace never portrayed a speck of a double life or sin, or portrayed any crude behaviour. She never missed going to church, but she had "travelled," which meant that she had consulted witch doctors to provide solutions to her family life. Grace was humble, kind and motherly. Though Anna was undergoing inner challenges, local concoctions had never crossed her mind. Yet, what Grace was telling her was a glaring reality in Mayenga.

Many women, out of desperation or proactive fear, were rumoured to travel far and wide to look for magical or love potions to manage, tame or reform their husbands. Some worked, they said, and some caused embarrassment and even death. In Mayenga alone, men loathed and seethed by a mere suspicion that a wife could be planning to administer to him a love potion. One could instantly banish her from the home, reform or else sing to her tune for the sake of his safety. It was that bad. Men had gone insane and lost lives through prescriptions of love potions. A woman was said to have been given a love concoction to feed to her roaming husband. The concoction turned out to be *datura stramonium*, a very poisonous weed that kills instantly. Another mixed a magical powder in her husband's meal. The effect turned out to be an embarrassment. The man opted to stay indoors, under his bed. He hated the sight of people. When the effect of the concoction subsided and he regained his senses, he had lost much, his job, dignity and a name in society. He banished the wife and remarried. Even then, he ensured that all his meals were cooked in his presence.

"It is not without cost," Grace pressed on. "A little cost is all it takes. But it's worth it."

"I need time to reflect on it," Anna answered sluggishly.

"It is all up to you. This is Mayenga, you know. Your destiny is in your hands," Grace shrugged off firmly.

When Grace excused herself to leave, it was not without a formidable challenge to Anna. Anna's marriage to Senta was a long-distance relationship that required more trust, communication and commitment. Though they were in constant contact over the phone, she only saw him when he visited home from Nairobi over the weekends. Even then, he was the eye of Mayenga; he was always busy with the projects of Mayenga or entertaining a chain of visitors in their home. He was engrossed in his passion: his desire to change the tides of Mayenga. More often, they talked on the phone and communicated openly about the children, their love or anything. This helped her understand how he was faring. It connected them. Through the phone, they poured out their hearts and Senta would promise a new present the next weekend.

She had no reason not to trust or suspect him of an extra-marital affair without finding out what was going on in his life. She felt that she had no reason to proactively approach the issue.

Senta always surprised her with a birthday card, a love letter, a unique present or an outing to blissful resorts. However lately, she noted, there was a change in his behaviour. He seemed in a hurry the entire time they were on the phone, and instead of the several calls he made in a day telling her of the challenges and experiences he was undergoing, they had reduced to one or two a day. He said that he was too engrossed in his work and projects to spare time for calls as it used to be the case. She cautiously noted this fact. "Grace could have a point. Senta could be having an affair with someone else if indeed what she tells me is true," she imagined. "No! Not the Senta I know!" she assured herself. "I'll talk to him the next time he is home. I'll share my fears and find out what might be happening. Is it that there is someone else he is seeing? Is it that there are other things that are troubling him apart from his passion for Mayenga, thus hindering our communication?"

That Friday evening, Senta came home from the city accompanied by friends. They conversed past midnight about issues affecting Mayenga. When he went to bed, he was too tired and had little time and energy to share with Anna. Anna recalled what Grace had told her during the day. Indeed Senta was having less time for her and with her.

When the cock crowed, there were elders and visitors outside their house waiting for Senta so that they could brief him about the projects of Mayenga. So, Senta woke up, hurriedly took a shower and left with the elders and the visitors. No sooner had Senta left with his team than Grace came in. She was inquisitive. "I heard him drive home last evening and I saw him drive away so early this morning."

"He has gone out, but I don't know where he has headed to," Anna informed her.

"He has left?" Grace wondered loudly shaking her head. "So early in the morning?"

"Without even informing me! True. My man has changed or he is obsessed with the projects. He is not the same man I married and this was not a marriage near my wildest dreams," Anna answered thoughtfully. "I'm at a loss," she sighed raising her hands.

"I told you," Grace continued, gesticulating with her hands. "I saw him with a group of women at the road chatting and laughing as I came in. I wish you could wake up. If you can't believe it, let's go and you will see for yourself."

Anna and Grace walked to the gate. A short distance away was a vehicle the county water coordinator used, and next to it was Senta's Trooper. They saw Senta with a group of three women who were actively involved in the Mayenga Water Project and some other people. One of the women was Millie, who was in a form-fitting pair of blue jeans and a white top. She was cracking jokes and laughing heartily as she took notes, and animatedly engaging Senta in a discussion. The other members joyfully applauded as Senta laughed heartily. Millie had a knuckle for jokes and a hearty extended laughter. Anna couldn't believe that Senta lived a double life.

"I can now see a lot of sense in what you are telling me," Anna sadly shook her head. "He can find the energy to joke and laugh with those women and idiots of Mayenga, yet he hardly spends enough time with me. Senta must be tamed by all means," she concluded.

Chapter Nine

The path to Ngweta village was pot-holed, muddy and slippery as a result of heavy downpours and a hilly terrain. It led uphill to a famous witch doctor who was renowned for her divinations and magical prowess. That morning, as Senta left the village for Nairobi, Anna and Grace set out to Ngweta. Their mission was to track and tame Vincent, as they were now persuaded that he lived a double life, not out of his own fault. It was caused by other women, among them was Millie, who had already plotted to wholly confuse and seize him.

"Anna, I'm telling you, with this woman you will never go wrong," Grace reassured Anna as they trudged through the sticky, mud and winding path. "He will sing to your tune and your life will be filled with success after success. You didn't marry him for Mayenga. Let the idiots of Mayenga shoulder their own problems."

"How did you come to know of this 'doctor', if I may ask?" Anna probed.

"Problems are a better teacher," Grace answered. "I had to travel, and this is not the only "doctor" I know. I've gone places and my eyes have seen things beyond your wildest imaginations. I've met church members who seek divinations and solutions to their problems. True, one can't put all his or her eggs in one basket. I once met someone and you wouldn't believe it, he went down on his knees pleading with me not to tell people that I had found him in a witch doctor's office. I promised! And I have kept the promise lid tight,"

Grace confided proficiently. "At one point, I had to have my womb blessed to bring forth sons. This was done to ensure that I had a son to gain respect and an heir to carry on our family name."

"Grace! You greatly amaze me a million times. You got your womb blessed? How can a womb be blessed by a witch doctor?" Anna was remarkably surprised. "I haven't heard of that." In a low tone while shaking her head, she said, "Grace, don't tell me you have out-of-marriage children in your house," Anna expressed surprise.

"None of it Anna. I've no speckled child in my marriage. That is against our customs. None of my children has been born out of wedlock. The doctor only had to bless my womb with charms," Grace explained. "You see, I had only had female children. I badly needed a boy to carry on the family name and to allow us to hold our heads up high. So, when I approached the doctor for a divination and a solution, his divination didn't point to anything wrong with me. 'Some women just have girls because their wombs aren't blessed or as a result of a curse,' the doctor candidly explained. I had to be sure I was on the right path. As a solution, I had to seek divination. His divinations ruled out a curse, and wanted my womb blessed. And being a doctor of divine powers, he prescribed charms for a small price, which I dutifully took. Consequently, my womb responded with a conception the same month. You know our first boy. He resembles his father, Mayaka," she laughed gently tapping Anna's back.

"That's strange. I have never heard of this in my life," Anna said. "In my biology class, I was taught that the sex of child is determined by X and Y chromosomes and not blessing of wombs. The X chromosome is donated by a mother and the Y chromosome by a father to bring forth a son. However, I need to admit that this world is dissimilar, with people of diverse beliefs and ways of perception."

"This is Mayenga! With the witches of Mayenga, anything is possible," Grace defensively said. "You have to be privy to it to survive."

Finally, they arrived at a homestead secured by a cacti fence and bold rocks. There were three grass-thatched huts in the compound. In front of the main house and to the left side, were a fenced kraal, a granary and a livestock resting field. Several chickens roamed freely, scratching and pecking from the earth, and beside them were several turkeys menacingly raising their feathers as the two women made their way into the compound. An old woman sat on a stool gently working with a mortar and pestle.

"I knew you were on the way here the moment you started your journey and that is why I never moved out of the home to the forest to replenish my herbal stock," said the plump, elderly, female witch doctor, dressed in a black *kitenge,* seated outside her house crushing dried herbs in a mortar using a long black pestle. "I don't sleep when I know my visitors are on the way."

Momentarily, Grace and Anna exchanged knowing and confident glances. The witch doctor had the divine power to foresee their coming.

The "doctor" shot up and led the two into a dimly lit hut to the left of the main house. "Come with me," she instructed in a pitched voice. Several lit candles mounted on darkened walls partially illuminated the hut. Inside, was a traditional three-legged stool, several containers with herbal concoctions on the floor, and dotted gourds hanging from the ceiling that had long darkened strands. At the centre of the hut laid her tools of the trade: a small pot, several shiny stones, cowry shells and an assortment of animal skins and skulls. They were placed on an old parched animal skin.

The "doctor" cleared her throat and began, "my children, what has brought you here this early morning?" the doctor considerately inquired as she motioned them to sit on the floor. The room was small and so they had to twist their legs to fit in it.

"Problems, doctor," Grace answered in a blotched voice.

"Aha. Problems," the "doctor" repeated. "I see. Problems toughen us if they don't break us. And that is why I'm here, to ensure they don't break you," she said in a convincing voice, smiling to herself. She held some stones on her palms and spread them methodically on the skin and pointed to one that had moved towards Grace. "I solved your problem. Now I can see you came here because of the young lady." The doctor looked at Anna. "She has a big problem on her hands. You're married with a husband staying in a big town?" the doctor compellingly inquired.

Anna wondered how this "doctor" knew that she was married and that the husband stayed in a big town. "It is true doctor," she answered in an ambivalent shiver.

"What is the problem?" the "doctor" probed gently.

"It is my husband. He has changed. He has no time for me..." Anna informed ecstatically her, sweating from her armpits.

"Stop!" the "doctor" interjected with her raised hands. "You must have a divination first to establish the root causes, and then we can know the best remedy to prescribe. A divination costs a hundred shillings."

Anna reached for her bag and pulled out a hundred

shilling note. She stretched her hand to give it to the doctor. "Here it is," she said shivering.

"Spit on it thrice and put it in the pot," the "doctor" instructed affectionately. "Then put your left hand on your chest and hold this gourd with your right hand. Pray silently to the spirits of the land, the waters and the sky. Tell them all your troubles and what you want them to do for you."

Meticulously, Anna put the note in the pot. Inside it was dark, but she could vaguely see several notes. They must have been from earlier clients. This reinforced her confidence in the "doctor." Then, dutifully she folded her hand on her chest and with a gourd in the other, prayed for some time. During that period, there was total silence in the room. She prayed for powers to enable her understand her husband, to get hold of him again, to ensure that all those women after him didn't have a chance to confuse him and for Mayenga to leave him alone!

The "doctor" spread the stones again. She studied them keenly, curiously pointing to each stone. "I can see your troubles, my daughter! You have no house and no home," she said sadly shaking her head, clicking and repeatedly snipping her fingers. "Young women like you have no idea how to go about this until troubles knock on their doors. Otherwise you could have prevented it a long time before it happened," she thoughtfully observed. "This brown woman here has already travelled to win his heart. She has already won him completely. Your man's heart is caged and divided, and he can't see a reason to have time with you," she shook her head again. "All he thinks about is her- this woman. Not you! And it's only a matter of time before you lose him completely."

"What is the way out, doctor?" Grace inquired hastily. "Is there a way out?"

"There is always a way out of this, my children," the "doctor" replied gently. "You can decide to get rid of the woman by instantly breaking her back without drawing any attention. This is expensive and you require a hundred thousand shillings and ten cents. The other option: you can completely detach his heart from her, and for this, you need only ten thousand shillings and ten cents. I prefer the latter. Though I'm a magician, I don't prefer shedding blood. I'm human too. And in any case, one who takes the first option must be over childbearing age; meaning one should never have children again because those hands have shed blood. You are still young. Aren't you? And you may want more children?"

"Yes, doctor," Anna replied.

"What you need is your man, and the woman can go roaming elsewhere with her shattered heart and life. She can even grow mad," the "doctor" assured them.

Millie had visited her home several times. Anna noted. She came in on the pretext of overseeing the Mayenga Water Project and often ended in her house where they shared lunches and chit-chats as women. Now she thought she knew her mission better. She was out for Senta, her husband. "The woman has got it wrong. She has played with fire. We must teach her a lesson," Anna retorted almost in a scream. "One who keeps going to other people's houses with bad intentions finally finds intestines at the hearth and leaves with them. Millie has found the intestines and she has to answer for their disappearance."

"She must be taught a lesson, that witch husband-snatcher," Grace firmly supported. "That is why she has refused to be married. If she is beautiful enough, why can't she get her own man? She should go mad, collecting papers and banana peels in the market places all in broad daylight, completely nude."

"That is my job," the "doctor" assured them, beaming. "Leave it to me, my daughters and by the end of it all, you will come back thanking me for a job well done. You will even come here with bundles of presents."

Anna paid ten thousand Kenya shillings and ten cents as instructed. She ritually spat on the money and dropped them into the pot before the doctor ordered her to remove all her clothing. With Grace's encouragement, she stood and hesitantly undressed one by one until she was completely nude. Using a sharp scalpel, the doctor proceeded to make incisions on her body. She started with her stomach, then thorax, her private area and head. She turned and made more incisions on her back and legs. It was painful, but Anna braved it all as it was worth the prize. She comforted herself. Blood oozed from the incisions as the witch doctor smeared them with a black and sharp penetrating powder, cursing the imaginary woman, setting Senta's heart free from her and re-binding it to Anna. "You, woman who snatches other women's husbands, why don't you look for yours," she said spitefully. "I curse you to madness; to roam completely nude in the market places, collecting waste papers and rags. I detach the heart of this lady's husband from you and rebind it to her and only her. He won't have any love outside his home!" the witch doctor earnestly declared. She gave Anna more medicine to mix in Senta's best meal.

"Take this, my daughter. I have seen you have suffered enough and you don't need to cry anymore. Tears were not meant for you. Mix it with your bath water and wash your body before he comes home. Once you bathe with it, don't greet anybody until you have slept with your husband. If you do, it won't work," the witch doctor instructed resolutely. She spat on the powder that was wrapped in a black polythene sheet and handed it to Anna. "Look for a chicken, and prepare a meal for him. Our men are lovers of chicken. When he comes home in the evening, receive him well with a hug, and then serve him his best meal: chicken and its soup. Before you serve him, mix this medicine in his soup. It must be done in secrecy. It is slightly bitter, but make sure the soup is a little spiced to conceal the bitterness. Let him enjoy the meal as you chat with him. Cheer him to eat but don't eat with him or taste the food. Once he eats, he will open up and tell you all his secrets if you want. Then go to bed, but the lights must be off in the bedroom so that he doesn't have to see the incisions. He can see them afterwards when the medicine has taken full effect."

Again the witch doctor handed the medicine in a small bottle to Anna. "This is your strength," she said smiling. "Keep it with your life. Be in touch and come to tell me of the new developments."

The witch doctor remained behind shaking her gourds and humming with their rhythms and bangles on her hands, as Anna put the medicine in her bag and exited with Grace coming behind.

As they left the compound, Anna had mixed feelings. She was bitter with Millie, whom she had trusted so much, but now Millie had snatched her husband. She was baffled at the witch doctor's meticulous ability to have a clue about her life, foresee her fears and unearth them and her willingness to solve them. The "doctor" was her best friend on earth, she concluded. She was happy that soon her tribulations would be behind her. "What does that woman, Millie, think she is? What does she have that I don't have?" Anna asked loudly holding her head and pulling the strands of her hair. "Money? Education? Beauty? A browner skin than mine? What's in that figure? She is shit!"

"She is proud because she went to school, but can't find a husband," Grace sarcastically snapped. "If she is so beautiful with a figure, why can't she find a husband? We shall see where her degrees, jobs and money will take her. We didn't go far in school, but we know more than she thinks she knows."

Chapter Ten

From Ngweta to Mayenga was a distance of almost fifty kilometres. One had to connect two vehicles to Mayenga through Kisii town. Before Anna and Grace boarded the second *matatu*, a Nissan from Kisii to Mayenga, Anna bought two hens and a sachet of crushed peppers at the market as instructed by the "doctor". On their way to the bus stage, they met Millie who was carrying files on one hand and a black handbag hanging from her shoulder. She was in the company of the county water engineer, several women leaders and other workshop participants. They were coming from a water project workshop held in Dados Hotel, Kisii, that day, in which Mayenga Women's Group Water Project was a show case of a successful community initiative, mobilisation and implementation of projects in the region. Millie was excited to see Anna, who was one of the Mayenga Women's Group leaders and one of the invitees for the workshop. However, Anna had not attended the workshop and in Millie's wits, she had a reason that could have hindered her attendance.

"Anna and Grace, my friends of Mayenga Water Project," Millie called out excitedly as she extended her hand to greet Anna. Millie was a confident and outgoing woman who dressed stridently. She had a sharp aptitude to match her flamboyance. "These are the brains and talents behind the Mayenga Water Project," she introduced them to the county water engineer and the participants as she looked at the engineer confidently. When she turned to look at Anna, Anna's hands were folded on her chest leaving

Millie's hand floating in the air. Further, Anna was staring at her menacingly and with a sarcastic smirk on her face. Millie was surprised at what she saw on Anna's face and that Anna could ignore her greetings and gaze at her threateningly in the presence of her boss and guests. She couldn't understand the developments. The water engineer was even more taken aback as he knew Anna at a personal level. "Is there anything wrong?" Millie asked Anna apologetically, as she extended the floating hand to Grace. Grace greeted her half-heartedly and facing the opposite direction, without uttering a word. "I expected Anna at the workshop. Anyway, we shall sort out any issues later," Millie commented, playing down the matter as the pair walked away to board a Nissan and head home.

"This is not the kind Anna, the wife of our friend Senta, I've known for long," the county water engineer remarked to Millie. "Did you offend her at any time?"

"I'm at a loss, boss. I was with her yesterday, we chatted, had lunch in her house and she even escorted me to the stage. She promised to be in the workshop today. I don't understand or have anything to say," Millie threw her hands up in despair. "Boss, even if she has any issue with me, this is not the way to approach it. I don't understand," Millie said shaking her head. "We better leave it at that. The world has issues and people. We're better off discussing matters that can take us somewhere." Millie brushed off any discussion on the matter, though internally she was troubled.

That night, as Anna lay in her bed, she couldn't afford not to reflect at the scene at Kisii town. She saw Millie walking to her in what appeared to be a pretentious show, extending her hand and pretending to be her best friend. She wasn't a fool, she reasoned.

Behind her back, Millie carried a double-edged sword, and with the other hand, goodies to deceive her and snatch her man. "No way!" she screamed pulling her hair and hitting her head on a pillow several times. "That witch had the audacity to greet me. Me! Eeh!" Anna fumed as she repeatedly beat her chest with her fist, "I'm Anna, the daughter of Chief Mogi. I swear by my mother, she is cheating herself. I let her hand float in the air as everybody watched to shame the devil. I don't care. I have her medicine. She will know me whether I wasn't circumcised, and whether women never sang for me in a morning."

Chapter Eleven

It was long past midnight as Vincent lay awake in bed in his apartment in Nairobi, staring blankly into space. No sooner had he slept than he had a horrible nightmare that astounded him. In the dream, he had gone home as usual over a weekend to visit his family and inspect his passion: The Mayenga Water Project. He was all alone as he walked to the tanks one early morning when he came face to face with a herd of mating dogs. They fiercely barked at him. He tried to scare them away with a walking stick, but they were menacingly hard on him. He tried to run away screaming, calling for help, but a determined neighbour's dog bit him on his leg from behind. He screamed louder, attracting the attention of the villagers. The villagers rushed to his rescue, but by the time they arrived several dogs had bitten him. Mecha, who was destroying birds' nests in his farm nearby, came in last, and even then he stood far as his faith was understandably known. He had nothing to do with dogs or any other animals. But then, he should have rushed in to chase away the dogs and save him. Something is wrong with his faith, Senta concluded. He must change and mend fences with neighbours to gain acceptance and stay well in the community.

When he woke up, he was sweating from all over his body. It was a bad dream, he admitted, but dreams are normal when one is exhausted, he justifiably reasoned.

A story was repeatedly told in Mayenga about Mecha and a cat. Many rats had invaded his house and had become a menace. As a solution, his wife Moraa acquired a cat and brought it home. Mecha was not at home when she arrived with the cat. When he came and found it enjoying a meal of milk, he admonished *nyachieni,* and in a rage took a machete and cut it into pieces as Moraa helplessly watched. To ensure he did not touch its blood or carcass, he cautiously wrapped the pieces in a polythene bag and left with them with the offensive machete. Nobody knew where he dumped the cat's carcass and the machete, but it was said that he dumped them far away from his home as he had gone for a long time. When he returned, he was haggard and panting. He made it clear to Moraa that his faith had nothing to do with animals, which the Almighty Almighty had cursed for disobeying him.

When the Water Project started, all women participated except Moraa. Men joined in and contributed, but Mecha and Moraa blatantly said that they could not associate or join hands with non-believers, meaning those they did not worship with. When the taps flowed with water, people swore that Mecha, Moraa, Morwabe and Nyamwanda could not use the water as they had not participated in the project. Senta saw a lot of animosity towards the couple. It took his intervention for Moraa to be allowed to get water from the taps.

As he was reflecting on the dream, his cell phone on his bedside rang. He took it and looked at the caller on the screen display. It was Millie. It was around three o'clock, and though they talked frequently on the Mayenga Water Project and shared chit-chats, Millie had never called him at night. She could be having a pressing issue she wanted to share or something was disturbing her, he reasoned. He pressed on the receiver and put the phone close to his ear.

"Hello, madam," he called out jovially.

"I'm quite alright," Millie replied and in a tensed tone of urgency proceeded. "Excuse me sir for calling you at this ungodly hour. I found the need to," she apologised profusely.

"You're most welcome, madam. Is there anything I can help with?" Senta interjected in a malleable voice.

"Indeed there is, my comrade," Millie now answered in a gentle and rather composed voice. She had not slept a wink that night after the incident with Anna in Kisii town, which had greatly embarrassed her and left her bruised internally. She had neither taken supper nor relaxed. She was tensed and confused with her mind racing to recall in every detail where she had wronged Anna or Grace. She knew Anna on a personal level, having been a regular visitor to their house in her Water Project mission at Mayenga. Though Senta had introduced them, she was closer to Anna than him, and they usually had chit-chats as women. Often, she dealt with Senta at an official level. At one point, Anna had jokingly encouraged her to have her own house, meaning she wanted her to be married. It meant Anna was concerned about her welfare too. In her last visit to their home, Anna had prepared for her a sumptuous lunch; a meal for esteemed visitors. They had sat and chatted and laughed for close to three hours. Anna had congratulated her for her aptitude and sharp dressing. "You dress like a princess going to catch the moon," Anna had teased her. She believed in being neat and ethical as part of her job enhancement. When she excused herself to leave, Anna had escorted her to the road with a gift of vegetables and fruits. "This is yours," she had said. "If there were children in your house, I would have given you more," Anna had teasingly remarked with a gentle friendly tap on her back. And then she had assured her that she would attend the workshop. Now she could not understand what had happened. Maybe, she reasoned, Senta could have a clue to the new development and be bold enough to offer her a hint.

Immediately, she got to her house from Kisii town, she had called Anna several times, but Anna's cell phone went unanswered. Truly, she could not recall doing anything that could have offended Anna. As a trained community officer, she knew that her strength in her work laid in maintaining a good rapport, honesty, integrity and upholding high ethical standards to the stakeholders. Only then, she could win the trust and confidence of the stakeholders to succeed in her projects. She couldn't fathom compromising it in any way. Now, Anna and Grace had written her off and eroded her confidence before her boss and other stakeholders. "No. Anna must be sick or something," she fussily concluded.

"Mister Senta, I've a burning issue that I would like us to share. I've carefully thought over it. I didn't want to involve you at the start, but now I have to. I'm a troubled woman." Millie started to recount in utter decorum.

"I will be glad if I can help," Senta urged her on.

"Forgive me if I'm intruding into your privacy and marriage," she politely excused herself. In a deep sigh, she began to narrate. "I've a lot of respect for you and I've no ill-intentions whatsoever. Today, I met your wife at Kisii town. She was in the company of her friend Grace. I had expected Anna to attend the Water Project workshop, but she conspicuously missed out, even after she had assured me just the previous day that she would attend. I was in the company of my boss and other stakeholders when I extended my hand to greet her and she ignored it and greatly embarrassed me. She stared at me threateningly. I've taken stock of myself, and I've no reason to say I ever crossed her path. It appears something is wrong, and I thought that you could have some insight into what is happening," Millie concluded with modesty.

"That's unimaginable! You say she didn't attend the workshop?" Senta asked in a surprised tone. "I talked to her in the evening and she said that that was the best workshop she ever attended."

"If she was there, then I didn't see her," Millie replied gently. "I'm concerned. It is unlike her. She could be stressed or sick. Please, take it upon yourself to ensure she is alright, sir. This mustn't put a wedge in your family. I beg." Millie had a way of communicating her points without causing apprehension. She was courteous and official at the same time when dealing with clients. She had a lot of respect for Senta as she had worked with him hand-in-hand in mobilising women towards the Water Project, and men had seen the need and joined them in digging trenches, laying pipes and diverting some water to the tanks while letting the streams follow with opulence. Thus, she had quietly put Senta in the front to gain access to Mayenga in what was quietly known in official circles as the stubborn Mayenga. Many officers had given up on Mayenga to a point of proscribing it. The credit of the project had been sliced into two. In her job as a county water coordinator, she was seen as a hero who had made in-roads to an unyielding village that many officers approached with profuse pessimism and caution. She had managed a successful eye-catching water project. In reward, she had sliced and eaten her own cake by moving two grades ahead. At the village level, Senta was seen as a hero who had conceptualised, initiated and overseen the project, and he was referred to as "the eye of Mayenga," meaning that he was able to see what they could not see. The trickle-down effect was felt all over Mayenga and the entire county, and the perception about Mayenga had started to change. So, she had no reasons to sever the mutual bonds between Senta and herself.

Senta could not understand what was happening. Millie had told him that she could not understand Anna, and Anna was actually in Kisii town fifty kilometres away from home when she was supposed to attend the workshop as a lead participant. Anna had told him over the phone nothing about Millie. She had even congratulated her and was upbeat about the workshop facilitators, referring to the workshop as the best she ever attended. Now, who was fooling who? Was it Millie, the overzealous county water coordinator, or Anna, his trusted and loving wife, the mother of his children?

Despite staying apart, he and Anna had undoubtedly built a strong trust and a communication that had not only created strength in their marriage but made their bonds very cordial. He had always thought that he understood her. His desire to take their relationship to enviable levels was always intense, but now he didn't know what was happening. Senta was left pondering. "I left home in an upbeat mood. I had an enjoyable weekend with Anna despite the many visitors and a busy schedule. Our marriage has been the envy of our friends and neighbours. Something is wrong," he copiously concluded.

Senta thanked Millie for her forthrightness and promised to get the root cause of Anna's extraordinary behaviour. However, he did not go back to sleep after these alarming revelations. He was a troubled man. Very early in the morning he called Anna, "Anna my sweetie. How was the night? Is there anything the matter?"

"My sweet husband! I tell you, I had the most magnificent night. I slept soundly and dreamed about you. Are you okay?"

"I'm okay, but I had a troubled night. I had a bad dream. The dogs of Mayenga bit me in my dream. And Mecha, in his characteristic manner, refused to save me."

"That was just a dream, my dear. Dogs can't hurt the eye of Mayenga when I'm there, and when they drink his waters!" Anna said in an assuring intonation.

"You said the workshop was the best you ever attended?" Senta snubbed. "Dados Hotel prepares the best meals in town. You know. It's one of the best hotels in the county, with excellent conference facilities."

"The best workshop held in my life," Anna said in a giggle. "You shall see the notes when you are home."

"What was the theme of the workshop?"

"As usual," she replied. "Clean water."

"The county water coordinator participated?" He probed further.

"That woman has become too proud of late. She is such a bore and a show-off in those body-forming outfits. People don't like her. She just sat," Anna replied rather unenthusiastically.

"She is the officer in charge and has done a lot for the Mayenga Water Project. She coordinates the project, ensures timely testing and treatment of water and repairs of the systems when they fail. I've a lot of respect for her," Senta corrected her. "She links the project with the donor funding..."

"Can we talk of something apart from that woman?" Anna interjected angrily.

"Well, she is an officer of noble standing and of amiable character. What would you demand this time, honey?" Senta did not want the issue to spoil their morning. So he switched the topic tactfully.

"The stars," Anna joked laughing heartily.

"I'm not on a journey to space. Fish fillet and a surprise for the weekend can do?" Senta suggested.

"Whichever pleases you, darling?"

The discussion ended without a long chit-chat unlike before. Anna's replies had been brief and closed ended. Millie had said she was not the same Anna she knew. He partially concurred with her.

Senta called Millie that morning. Millie was excited and overzealous as she briefed him about the workshop. It was held in Dados Hotel and the venue was excellent. She was one of the lead facilitators. The theme was: Mayenga Women Group Water Project; a showcase of a successful community initiative, mobilisation and implementation of projects in the county. She confirmed again that Anna did not attend the workshop and if she did, then she did not see her. She intelligently avoided discussing the unpleasant incident with Anna the previous day as she did not want to put a wedge between Senta and Anna over an issue she did not comprehend. Senta noted that Millie had etiquette and decorum commensurate to an officer of her standing.

Chapter Twelve

The weekend that followed, Senta had a busy schedule in Mayenga. A field day had been proposed by the county water coordinator as an idea he had initially floated. Many participants were expected to attend. The theme had tentatively been suggested as "fighting poverty through harnessing available resources." It was fully financed by the county with Millie as the link. The Mayenga Water Project had propelled the village to greater fame. It was a case study on how a people can conceptualise, initiate, and mobilize themselves and resources to achieve clean drinking water. Other villages had started copying the idea and were mobilising themselves and pulling resources together to have clean drinking water from the rivers and streams within reach. Already a documentary film had been done on the project and aired on television and radio channels.

Senta was in Mayenga a day earlier to assist with the preparations for the field day. He arrived at the village on a Friday afternoon. On the way home from the market centre, a group of drunken youth had helped him push his vehicle, which had gotten stuck in the muddy road. Then, they escorted him all the way to his house singing and chanting in praise of him. Their intentions were to get his attention and get kickbacks for their service, which they could use for their entertainments.

"Allow me to ask you, my good friends," Senta posed to them considerately. "Why do you young men drink so much?" Each of them had an answer.

"Me, I drink because I have no job," one said.

"I drink because I'm bored."

"I drink hard to feel high."

"I drink to kill the stresses of life."

"I drink because my friends do."

"I drink to retaliate against my parents who refused to pay my fees and don't understand me."

"I drink because my parents drink."

"Well, for now," Senta said, "these may appear to be valid excuses, but they won't solve your long-term problems." Then he asked them about their levels of education. None had gone beyond primary school except Peter, who had made it up to fourth form. Even then, he had a miserable score. Some had noble dreams of what they wanted to become and others had no idea. They wanted to have white-collar jobs. They wanted to be pilots, soldiers, police officers, teachers and so on. The dreams were good, but were grossly misplaced. "How do you expect to be a pilot or a doctor, when you dropped out of school in primary?" he asked gently. None could answer him. "It's not practicable. Boredom and stress are part of life. Our parents have lived their lives, and it's upon us to map out ours. Allow me to challenge all of you to wake up to the current realities! Find something to do, and do it well while you work for your dreams. You can even infuse your energy in community projects." They blamed the government, their leaders and their parents for their state of affairs.

"What we're today is as a result of the sacrifices of yesterday," Senta advised them. "What we shall be tomorrow shall be the results of the choices we make today. The past is behind us, but we hold the keys to our future. The Water Project is a case on how hard work can make a change. The situation in Mayenga didn't start yesterday. It stretches ways back, and its effects are felt into this generation, and if nothing is done the future will charge us harshly. The way forward is to change and accept our situation, map the way out of our miseries by identifying our talents and what we can do best, then work harder to achieve our goals. Through that, those who will come after us will have a better life. I know Peter is a good football player but he hasn't put it into use."

The youth listened attentively and left the home challenged. They had all along blamed others for their state of affairs without doing any self-evaluation. Some had even felt that education was not necessary as Nyamwanda had made it to riches without any basic education. Nevertheless, they were now aware that they could make a change in their lives through hard work and focus.

Mecha and Moraa, an elderly childless couple in Mayenga lived a life different from that of many in the village. Their childlessness was a subject of much gossip, innuendo and speculation. Several myths were advanced to explain the causes behind it: evils spirits, witchcraft, curses and their own faith in the Almighty Almighty.

Moraa was thin and gaunt with sunken eyes, but she exuded a jovial demeanour. She was the opposite of Mecha who was bulky with a large belly and a mean decisive stare. They were a poor couple, producing all their foods in their *shamba* with none to sell. They were staunch believers in their faith and had little in the form of earthly possessions. Earthly possessions, they said, had no meaning to them as they were only passengers in a train passing on earth to a place where the Almighty Almighty had prepared a magnificent place for them. In Mayenga, they were the only ones who subscribed to the sect that had no physical building for a church.

The couple had little association with people except those they worshipped with who often congregated at their house. Here they prayed, clapped hands, drummed, danced and sang all nightlong, casting "the devil", *nyachieni*, into an inferno and asking the Almighty Almighty to take control. Their faith remained a mystery to many villagers.

They never attended the chief's *barazas*. They never ate meat or any animal products, preferring vegetables and fruits. Thus they did not rear any animals in their homestead. Further, they did not shake hands with people except those they worshiped with. Instead, they acknowledged greetings by clapping their hands or nodding their heads, but greeted their fellow worshippers with long embraces and hugs. They never shaved their hair and their heads were always covered in black caps or veils with red crosses on the fore centre, which had the words "Almighty Almighty" inscribed on them. They always walked with big crosses and their necks were full of rosaries. Always in flowing black robes, and covered heads, they sang praises with frenzied exploits to a god, Almighty Almighty, people did not understand. When sick, they could not visit a hospital, but only prayed and praised their god, commanding him to bind and chase the tormenting spirits of sickness. Their lifestyle largely remained a question to the village. Though they often hosted fellow believers who were strangers to the village, they lived in isolation from the rest of villagers who did not conform to their faith and very few villagers, if any, had ever entered their house.

Mecha and Moraa were jumping, clapping and singing outside their mud-walled, iron-roofed house and admonishing *nyachieni,* when Senta visited them in the afternoon. Mecha wore a tattered black gown flowing down to his ankles. His head was covered in a black cap with a red cross and the words "Almighty Almighty" ingrained at the fore centre. His neck had several rosaries made of beads and cowry shells, and both of his hands had several bangles lining from the wrist to the elbow. Moraa was dressed in a similar manner only that her head was covered in a black veil and her hands had fewer bangles.

Mecha was in a frenzied fit, frantically beating the air with his cross, spitting and howling insults to the imaginary *nyachieni*. Surprise was written on their faces when they saw Senta walking into their compound through the debilitated timber off-cuts gate. As if they had seen danger, they stopped singing at once, and in utter silence stared at him fixedly and quizzically as if ready to take flight.

Senta broke the silence by greeting them. "Hello uncle and aunt."

After a long silence, Mecha opened his mouth. "Welcome, my son. What has brought you here?" Mecha spoke in a quiver as Moraa stood holding her cross next to her chest. "You have never visited us before."

"Uncle, I have come to greet you," Senta explained extending his hand out, but Mecha clapped repeatedly as Moraa joined in.

"I accept your greetings," Mecha replied in a hyperactive voice.

"I haven't seen you for a long time and my heart burns with a desire to talk to you," Senta said. They were both standing. "Maybe we can sit so that we can share?"

Moraa went into the house and brought a wooden arm-chair. The couple sat on an off-cut bench fixed outside their house while Senta sat on the wooden chair. Even then, Mecha ensured that there was a clear distance between him and Senta. Senta was a non-believer in his faith. He was aware that few people had ever entered the couple's house, except those who shared in their faith. Their compound was securely fenced by a shrub fence with only one way to the road uphill. Senta's intentions were a deliberate move to make the pair see the need to coexist in the community irrespective of their faith, and that their solitude was a counterproductive venture.

"Uncle and aunt, I love you and I want to share with you quite frankly as your son," Senta began. "You come after my father. So, I'm also your son, and therefore, I'm obliged to have a say where it matters. I've nothing sinister," Senta posed as he surveyed them keenly. The couple's eyes maintained quizzical expressions. "But I don't really envy your lifestyle. If nobody has ever said it before, forgive me to say so." He looked at them again. Moraa was very attentive, but Mecha appeared distant with a mean resolute stare. "I'm not happy with the way you live in exclusion from the rest here in Mayenga. There is nothing wrong with one having a belief or a faith, but there is something absolutely wrong if these can entirely isolate one from the rest of the community. Uncle, you can't afford to live in isolation and expect peace and prosperity. In a way, these are God's extended blessings. We need each other to solve our problems, uncle and aunt."

Suddenly, Mecha bolted up hysterically and started jumping, clapping and praying like one possessed by some strange powers. "Blala blala. The Almighty Almighty, the devil, *nyachieni* is our enemy number one."

Senta stared at him for a moment with askance written over his face. He could not fail to notice a man "drunk" with strange indoctrination or who lost his track a long time ago. "Uncle, forgive me if I've offended you, but it is for your good and the good of Mayenga, if you afford to listen," Senta tried to sound rational.

"Can't you listen?" Moraa interjected angrily. "Our son has a point. Nobody has ever visited us, but our son has braved to see us. Accord him some respect." Mecha started to speak in tongues. After a while he slowly calmed down. He sat on the bench and was now attentive, but with a distant stare.

Senta continued. "When we initiated the Water Project, it was a noble idea for all the people of this village. It was meant to serve all of us and everybody participated. Even if you didn't participate or contribute towards it for some reason, we understood. Now, you are able to drink clean and treated water from the taps. It has reduced aunt's load to the fall downhill and reduced water-borne infections in Mayenga," Senta ideally explained in a gentle voice. "Uncle, I would love to see you happy, working and moving forward together with the rest of the community for your good and the good of Mayenga. Doing so, I guess doesn't contravene your faith and the reason for our coexistence."

"My son, I see a lot of sense in what you are saying. But, there is no point in the things of this world as the world is a dead shell and is soon coming to an end. The Almighty Almighty high up there has already prepared a better place with a better life for us," Mecha said, pointing to the sky. "Even if I live or die, my destiny is to the Almighty Almighty. My faith is greater than all these things of the earth. Are you willing to accept the Almighty Almighty? I'll pray and baptise you right now." Mecha stood up, acted as if he was preaching and ready to lay his cross on Senta's head. "Are you ready to accept the Almighty Almighty to rule your life right now and leave all the things of this world?" he asked ecstatically, gesticulating with his black thorn, *Muma*, the Bible in one hand and a cross in the other, raised high over his head.

Senta sprung up and moved a little distance away from Mecha. "Uncle, everything has its time. I may wish to know more about your faith if you bothered to listen to me," he pleaded. However, he realized that the whole of Mecha's life revolved around his faith and nothing else made sense. He decided to let the matter rest at that.

Senta left Mecha's home satisfied that he had done his part. Moraa escorted him to the gate as Mecha sang and clapped with his hands raised up. As Moraa clapped as a sign of goodbye to Senta, she said, "my son, I've nothing wrong with what you are doing. I wish I could be part of the team of the Mayenga Women's Group, but my faith, the faith your uncle introduced to this home, won't allow me. We women have to follow our men to maintain peace. Your uncle isn't the same the moment we accepted the Almighty Almighty to rule our lives. I too don't understand him," she explained emphatically. "It all started when we couldn't have a child. After successively trying several ways, but we were unsuccessful, we joined the faith that promised a solution. Though we didn't achieve our intention, we have never looked back. Never!" Her eyes were imploring and shiny with tears. Senta couldn't miss the loneliness and subtleness in her heart.

"Take heart, aunt," he comforted her. "All will be well, finally."

"Because of our solitude," she continued, "people say we're witches. We're not! We are good people. Our whole heart is unto the Almighty Almighty," Moraa said calmly and with subtleness. "In the end, we shall triumph and go to the place where we shall have a better life."

As he walked back to his house, Senta reflected on the moments he had spent with Mecha and Moraa. Mecha was either insane or overzealous with his faith. He could not quite understand him. Mecha did not see reality or anything good in life. Even his own wife did not understand him. He was known in Mayenga as Character because of his uniqueness. Mecha spent much of his time removing and destroying birds' and rats' nests from his compound. All animals, he claimed, had contaminated blood and had sinned against the Almighty Almighty. Therefore, he had nothing to do with them. A neighbour's animal that strayed to his compound could end up with terminal spinal or head injuries. Because of this, neighbours had resorted to tethering their cows with two ropes just in case one snapped and the animal strayed into Mecha's compound. They reasoned that it was worth it to lose a rope rather than a cow.

The odd couple and Nyamwanda had nothing to do with the community projects. Even with his big store in the market where he dealt in skins and hides, and financial muscle, Nyamwanda just like the couple lived in a world of his own.

"A strange world this Mayenga!" he observed, shaking his head.

Chapter Thirteen

At the entrance to his compound, two elders who were instrumental in mobilising and disseminating Senta's ideas in the village were standing waiting for him. From the look of their eyes and posture, they had been waiting for some time, Senta noted.

He greeted them jovially. "My good elders," he called out. "You're my comrades at arms in Mayenga. As usual, I expected you to be seated in the house taking a cup of tea," Senta remarked as he ushered them into his compound.

One elder who was bold and looked disturbed held his chin and said, "No! *Omogambi*, chief, we can't hide this from you. Men don't hide their nakedness from other fellow men. We've to tell you the truth," he said thoughtfully. "Something is wrong with your house. We were here one hour ago. Your wife, Anna, was in the house when we knocked! She opened the door for us. And without a word, retreated and disappeared inside leaving us seated in the living room. She didn't even welcome us in with a glass of water, but we welcomed ourselves. It isn't our culture to sit in a house without the owners. No!"

"She has been a jovial, kind and lovely mother," the other elder interjected. "This was unlike her. For this reason, we shall finish our business right here at the gate for today."

No convincing words could soften the elders' stance. So, they discussed business right there. They detailed how they had sensitized people about the upcoming field day and how people were enthusiastic about it. For that, Senta paid them a little for their service. They left as Senta entered his compound, but with a word of caution to him. "Women are interesting creatures. We've them, and yours isn't different. We're not telling you to go fight, but take care!"

The main door to his house was closed as he walked to the house, but Anna, immediately opened it as Senta stood at the doorstep. "My honey, how I miss you," she hugged, kissed him and jumped onto his chest like a little baby.

Senta held her and carried her in his arms. "Baby, my love for you is stronger than it was yesterday. I live because you do," he flattered her. "You're the most beautiful woman I've ever set my eyes on"

"Really?" Anna remarked shyly with a beaming face.

"Your face is ever radiant, with such warm smiles, a big heart and your eyes are ever full of understanding." Senta was full of praises for Anna. "You've whole-heartedly supported my efforts to make a difference in Mayenga. You know, one can't move forward alone and have peace in a village like this. Through your efforts, we're creating peace and prosperity for this home and for society. You can't live in the midst of want, close your eyes and expect rewards. If all of us did a little to change society, society would be a better place to spend our eternity. People need to be empowered through information so that they are able to create positive changes in their lives," he said. "My dear, do you feel the bullets of desperate eyes hitting your heart? It pains me. Do you see a longing of the youth for a better life?" Senta sounded rhetorical. "When their dreams are locked in self-pity, and insulated beliefs because few care about their plight and future?"

"I do," she answered.

"I care so much, and that is why I do all these things. That is why I can go to uncle Mecha's house against all odds. I grew up in this village and I wish to see it prosper. They long for a better life but have no way out. They have no inspiration. They are yolk in an egg shell, and have no powers to wriggle to break the membrane and come out of the shell to a new beginning."

"Mayenga must have bothered you to a point that you're growing thin. Today you have spent a whole day in the service of Mayenga and I guess you must be very hungry," Anna said politely. "As we talk, you can be enjoying your super to quench the hunger and replenish your energy."

Anna had earlier prepared a sumptuous supper of chicken and chapattis, packed it in two porcelain pots and placed it on the dining table. The aroma from it was appetising. She carefully served it to Senta with a cupful of chicken soup. "Unfortunately, I've had my super," she excused herself. "Today, you will have to eat alone as I cheer you up," Anna said as she served the food. "I need to see you put more flesh on your bones in order for me to gain respect as a wife who knows how to cook for and feed her man. Women are laughing at me and doubting my cooking because you aren't adding weight," she cracked a jock which Senta returned with an apologetic smile.

"Tell them the problem is me. I've refused to put on weight," he tried to amuse her. "The meal is delicious, only that there is more pepper than usual," Senta commented as he sipped the soup.

"Curry accidentally fell into the soup. Next time I'll be more careful, my dear," Anna apologised unreservedly. "Trust me; this chicken is an exchange for your fish fillet. I swallowed the fillets mouthful," she joked cheering him to take more soup.

Senta informed Anna about his visit to Mecha's house. "My uncle has gone crazy. I guess," he remarked. "He can't be taken seriously. I'm of the opinion that he lost his path long ago and the faith is just a cover-up or has accelerated his condition. Even aunt Moraa doesn't appear to understand him."

Anna concurred that Mecha was not himself. "I wish you could see the village children imitate him in their little games. Boys compete with their little crosses, some calling themselves Mecha, others, Character; and girls, Moraa. They march in files with enthusiasm shouting, 'I've nothing to do with animals. All animals have sinned against the Almighty Almighty. I'm going to the palace to have a better life.' You'll laugh till your ribs hurt. Ironically, when Mecha sees them marching and singing, he stands a distance with his arms akimbo to watch them."

"Ideally, Mecha needs to see a psychiatrist." In an afterthought, he posed, "dear, tell me, has anybody come to see me here while I was away?"

"Nobody has come to this house today," Anna replied firmly. "I've been here all along."

"You're damn right?" he asked again.

"Hundred per cent sure," she confirmed.

"That is a big percentage," he posed and took a deep sigh. "As I was coming in, I happened to meet two elders at the entrance. They said you snubbed them," he said frankly but politely. "They were rather unhappy at the way you supposedly treated them."

"Me? Anna? Ee, those elders are crazy. Have I ever snubbed anybody or have you ever heard anybody complain about me all these years we have lived together as husband and wife?" Her voice was high and trembling in rage.

"My wife, I don't mean anything bad, but I'm becoming concerned. I'm not snooping around or failing to trust you, but of late I'm getting complaints that are contradictory. I'm told you didn't attend the workshop and you embarrassed Millie in front..."

Anna rose in haste and with anger written on her face at the mention of Millie. "Excuse me! Stop mentioning that witch," she shouted at the top of her voice. "Stop talking about her in the same way you stopped suckling your mother's teats. I embarrassed Millie? How lovely you pronounce her name." In an afterthought, she moved closer to Senta. This time in a lower and lovelier tone, and said, "My husband, I love you so much. Don't listen to people who want to put a wedge between us. You come first in my life. I hope I do in yours."

As a family they had had differences of opinion, but he had never seen Anna get so unreasonably worked up. She had never shouted at him the way she did. Something was terribly wrong. He felt it in his veins. "I need to talk to her when she cools down," he reasoned. "Anyway," he shrugged with a sigh of relief. "Let's put that aside, and discuss about our life and children. My interest rests in my family. I want to see you happy and that happiness will help us move forward." After Senta had had his supper, they resigned to their bedroom for the night.

The bedroom was pitch-dark as the bulb had blown off. Anna explained. They slept holding onto each other and woke up late in the morning. Senta felt so tired to attend the field day preparations scheduled for that day. He felt sick and weak, and attributed it to the long journey to the village or malaria. His vision was blurred, and as Anna rose from bed, Senta could not fail to notice, though faintly, healing incisions all over her body, but he was too tired and sleepy to question the causes of the marks.

For the first time, Anna left him in bed sleeping. Grace had visited Anna that morning and they animatedly talked in low voices behind the house as Senta slept. "You did as the "doctor" instructed you?" Grace inquired.

"I followed the instructions to the letter. Today he hasn't gone to his projects to meet that witch," Anna confidently confided to Grace, with her arms akimbo and swinging her hips seductively. "He is in the house tamed by Anna, daughter of the Chief. I'll be as tough on him as the 'doctor' advised and he will know the daughter of Chief Mogi doesn't take challenges lying down like a defeated bull," she beat her chest.

They shared the joke in prolonged laughter repeatedly tapping their palms onto each other before Grace excused herself to leave.

Chapter Fourteen

Rumours were rife in Mayenga that Millie, the county water coordinator, was actually a husband snatcher. Her frequent visits to the village to oversee the Water Project were of no good but an extended mission to catch the eye of Senta. The way she dressed told it all: body-tight trousers, mini-skirts and see-through blouses to entice and impress him. Her boldness, to even climb up the water tanks like a man in the pretext of inspecting them, was calculative and intentional. People gossiped that she had succeeded in her mission, and was now coordinating his heart through remote magic. Senta, they said, did not want to spend a minute with his family because his mind and heart were already tamed by this woman. To meet her and spend time together, he had to come up with various projects where Millie was at the centre of activities. It was rumoured that she frequently travelled to Nairobi to spend time with him, and he had even secretly bought land in the fringe of Kisii town and built a bungalow for her. They said, Senta had already visited Millie's home on several occasions and completed dowry negotiations. What remained was the final celebration of their union through mandatory payment of the bride price to Millie's parents.

These rumours had coincidentally reached Millie. Initially, she had brushed them aside as meaningless, unfounded, cheap village gossip, peddled by idlers. She saw them as croaks of a frog in a river that couldn't scare or prevent cows from drinking the water. However, when she revisited the embarrassing episode with Anna in Kisii town, she felt hurt inside, noting that her conscience was beyond reproach. Then, in her duties at Mayenga, children had stopped playing at the sight of her and sang with one soloing and others joining in a chorus, "who knows how to snatch husbands? Millie! Who knows how to snatch husbands? Millie!" Her driver had quickly driven off from the scenes of the singing children at a breakneck speed to avoid further embarrassment. They sang loudly until the vehicle was off the bend. On the way, she was met with cold and questioning stares. These stares were from people who had given her support before, and had overwhelmingly appreciated her work. Her confidence and ego as a community worker were greatly put into question.

However, Millie had people on her side who appeared to feel for her pain and see things her way. Kundi was one of them. He was the acknowledged village innovator, and each time an officer came to Mayenga, he was inquisitive and eager to learn new ideas and experiment with them. After his grade cow had died, he had tried his hand in poultry and bee keeping. Now, Kundi was the sole supplier of eggs and natural honey to the entire market, raking in huge profits. He had little time for small talks and gossips. When Millie confided in him how troubled she was, he understandingly encouraged her not to let the matter overweigh her as it was the work of idlers and pessimistic people envious of her success. He invited her to his home to see his other new venture: a plot of tomatoes, bees and poultry. "With my bees, poultry and this, I've little time for petty gossips," Kundi said.

"They even say I've tamed *majini*, ocean fauna, and that is why my ventures haven't failed. But, I don't listen or allow these cheap talks to overweigh me. They see me working hard in my garden each day. I don't entertain idlers and gossipers. You can take the same stand," Kundi dutifully advised her.

In the office, workmates got wind that Millie had actually snatched someone's husband in the course of her work. Some gossiped behind her back and loathed the behaviour. Others had abhorrent questions written all over their faces. "How could she do such a thing as a community worker? Where is her work ethics or integrity?" They questioned. However, Millie's boss, the county water engineer was sympathetic. He knew Millie well, having worked with her for a long period of time. He envied her zeal for work, what she had done for Mayenga and by extension to the county water office. She was a rare talent in the public service, taking her work with enthusiasm and etiquette. The effect of her work was felt in what officers had called "the stubborn Mayenga", and had trickled to the entire region. She was the best water coordinator he had ever worked with. He reasoned that if one wants to kill a dog, one starts by giving it a bad name. He saw this as a work of malice to demoralise Millie, thus killing the water project. He took time to counsel and encourage her, and asked her to take time off work to relax from her hectic work schedule. Further, he recommended her for a full scholarship for further studies upon completion of her leave. The leave was to start after the Mayenga Field Day.

Millie was energised that at least there were those who appreciated what she did. This provided her with an opportunity to closely supervise the construction of her house in Kisii town.

Senta's father, Areba, had gotten wind that Senta had a secret wife. He had also noted Senta behaving strangely. He was withdrawn, avoided visitors, talked less, and had little time for Mayenga and his own projects. Instead, he preferred to spend his time at his house all alone sleeping. He would come home from the city over the weekend and not bother to ask how his parents were faring. So, his father went to his house and found him sleeping outside on the veranda behind the house. "My son, are you alright?" Areba inquired. "Men don't sleep in the day like brooding chickens. They have to move around to gather for the young ones. Even a brooding hen briefly comes out of her nest to look for food."

"I'm alright father. I'm only resting," Senta replied in a low tone as he extended his hand to greet his father. Evidently, he appeared weak and tired. His eyes were sleepy and distant, a sign of a troubled man.

"My son," he fondly and gently drew Senta's attention. "As your father, I'm greatly concerned about you," Areba said thoughtfully looking at him. "Rumours are doing around that you've another family somewhere and you've even built a house for her somewhere in Kisii town. And I, as your father, am not in the picture," Areba said gently. "I may not believe what is said because I understand our people and their ways of handling issues that don't concern them. If it's not true, don't allow it to stress you and put you down. Keep focused on what you're doing. Many people are happy about your projects, but some may not and will find ways to bring you down. Remember that every obstacle presents an opportunity for you. Every enclosure has an escape route," Areba counselled him as Vincent listened keenly. "And even if you decide to spread your wings and sow seeds like wild oats, what is wrong with that?" he asked authoritatively. "What does it concern them? A leader is more powerful and respected when he has more suckers emerging from his own stem. I'm more proud to have more grandchildren running around, not these two. In our times, our wives didn't 'lock their wombs' the way your generation is doing. They were even proud to suckle a new young one every season and have a co-wife as a helper."

"Father, men talk where it hurts. It's not about people. People don't bother me. Even Morwabe's sceptical, diabolic cynicism at the market about the projects can't. But my wife, Anna," Senta confided in low tone pointing to the house. "She has become a wound in my stomach. She has changed from the woman I met and married. She no longer has respect for me. Anna was the powerhouse, remember, and my goodwill ambassador in the village for my projects. Today she sees nothing good in them. She has unkind words for me, and argues vehemently over trivial matters. She calls me all sorts of names, names a man in his house doesn't deserve," Senta said slowly shaking his head. "Father, I don't have another wife. I have nothing to do with Millie; they say I have secretly married. Millie is a good professional who does her work with unmatched zeal. A rare talent one can find. Remember what she has done for Mayenga, yet she hails not from Mayenga. I feel sick inside. I don't know what's happening to me. I feel tired and my head aches. I keep dreaming of things I never dreamed about. I feel insecure and I've no interest in anything now." Again, he shook his head slowly. "Father, something is terribly wrong."

"My boy," Areba chipped in sympathetically. "You're a boy before me, though you've travelled and read widely," he said candidly. "As a man, I understand your troubles. Take heart my son, and be strong like *omotembe*, erythrocima tree, that survives through seasons to blossom with rose-pink flowers and is used to bless and curse. No man has ever waded through life without meeting challenges from time to time. Weak ones break, but tough ones don't allow a chance to break them. Let challenges make you stronger. Women are like that. They are a bark of another tree and hard to understand. Even your mothers are not angels. We only put up with them because of necessity. When you face challenges, son, don't quit. Don't despair. When life kicks you hard, let it kick you forward," he continued.

Senta stared at his father as he received the old man's counsel. "Sometimes, we don't conquer through brilliance. Men conquer through sustained persistence. Be persistent to the end, like a warrior defending his father's stool. One may despair when the sun is almost shining on him. It's true, a farmer can't dictate the sun to shine on his side to ripen his crops, but he can adjust his planting times so that he can have a harvest. Make capital out of the disaster and move on. Every obstacle is an opportunity and a chance to learn. When tomorrow comes, my son, it shall find you somewhere better." Areba stopped and stared distantly. "When you have an issue, discuss it with me. You used to consult a lot. Of late you don't.

Men don't hide their nakedness from other men. I'll be back to see you shortly."

Areba left Senta where he found him. The old man coughed and sneezed on his way to his house. "If my son was well, he could have heard that my cough is bad and brought me medicine even before I coughed twice," he murmured to himself.

Anna, who had been secretly listening to their conversation from inside the house rushed out and confronted Areba. "So, you're the one encouraging your son to marry? We shall see," she retorted.

Areba was surprised at the remarks. He had never exchanged words with his daughters-in-law and he had no reason to. Further, it was considered abominable to do so. He stood and stared at her apologetically. "My daughter," he said in a gentle voice. "You're my daughter-in-law, and our customs don't allow us to exchange words. Have some respect for me. There is a boundary of respect between a daughter and father that you're breaking," he said as he left coughing to his house.

Chapter Fifteen

Mayenga Field Day was solely organised by Millie, with no input from Senta. Vincent Senta, who had floated the idea neither attended the event nor sent a word of apology. He had initially lauded the idea as the best to create attitudinal changes and accelerate development in Mayenga and the county. He backed his argument with the fact that the Mayenga Water Project was the first of its kind to succeed in the region, and its trickle-down effects were felt in other villages. It had become a case study throughout the county, looking at how a community could initiate, mobilize, implement and successfully manage a project for their betterment. To encourage the project, donors supported it in terms of free water testing, treatment and repairs of the water equipments. This was coordinated through the office of the county water coordinator, where Millie was the officer in charge. However, the project was wholly owned and managed by the community. Hers was to ensure that the treatment chemicals were available, delivered in time and that the water was treated and was fit for human consumption; the systems were in sound state and she managed external communication with stakeholders to and from the project site.

However, Senta had grown cold midway and appeared to have no fire left for the projects he had passionately initiated. Even the theme for the event, "fighting poverty through harnessing available resources," was his brain-child. Millie had made in-roads to Mayenga through Vincent. Senta had been a useful link to the project women's group. He was a trusted leader. He had the enthusiasm, the charisma, empathy for the people and passion for the project. With his assistance, they had written a convincingly good proposal for donor assistance and inputs and it had yielded good results. With Vincent's disinterest in the community projects and the people talking ill and gossiping about her, she persisted on out of professionalism and passion for her work. In any case, this was the last assignment in Mayenga and she didn't want to burn any bridge. However, she reasoned that Senta had a good cause to keep away from Mayenga, perhaps giving room to the wanton fire to cool off naturally. Alternatively, he was disparaged by the damaging gossips and broken down.

Millie had avoided trips to Mayenga for a while. With her infrequent visits to the Water Project site, that day she noted in a tour to the site that some pipes were copiously leaking and some water tap knobs were missing, thus wasting treated water. Then Kundi had confided in her that the pump attendant was actually selling water treatment chemicals secretly at a throw-away price, under dosing the water and the watchman was never at the site to switch on and off the water pumps and lights in time. The level of tidiness was down. The management committee was appropriating for themselves the monthly proceeds meant to sustain the salaries of the workers. Men were jostling and fighting to take leadership of the Water Project. Morwabe was in the frontline. "The management team has eaten enough. Their time is up. It's our time now." This was his campaign slogan in the market, and coincidentally, he had pulled a crowd. Undeniably, the Mayenga Water Project had drastically gone down. However, there were those with a heart for the Water Project, and Kundi and Menge, remained some of them.

Before the field day kicked off, a group of elders sat at a corner discussing how Mayenga had benefited from Senta. "Truly, who is this man, Vincent Senta? Is he really the son of Areba who was once known to be a village drunkard? He is unlike Areba who doesn't associate a lot. We can't quite understand him. He is unlike our children in Mayenga," one piously said.

"He is like his grandfather," another said. "Don't you remember his grandfather? He could never slaughter a goat and eat it all alone. His tobacco was village tobacco. He was generous till the grave."

Another chipped in. "He is a well-read man with a heart for his people. He has travelled and has seen a lot outside Mayenga. He is interested in an elective seat. He has a lot of money to dish out. Why spend all that money and time on people if he isn't interested in a seat?"

"You're wrong. He has never hinted that he is interested in any elective seat. Perhaps his eyes trail to the future. You never know with people," another said shrugging his shoulders. "He is a conspicuous tall *omotembe* tree in the village of Mayenga. He is a God-sent Messiah for our people. Having been born to poor parents in a poor village, his interest is to make a difference and he is paying back in kind. He thinks well about us. When I lacked seeds for planting, I went to his house and told him that the season was passing without a single seed in my garden. He listened to me and asked, 'have you prepared your garden?' I hadn't prepared, so I told him, 'I'll prepare once I have seeds'. He advised me to prepare the garden first, and see him the weekend that followed. He reached into his pocket and handed me some 'tea.' I was profusely grateful as I had nothing in my pockets. The Saturday that followed I was by his door very early. When he saw me, he asked if I had prepared my garden, and

I assured him I had done so. He handed me a bag of seeds and fertiliser. 'Next season, you will have enough food and a surplus to sell, and buy your own seeds and fertiliser for planting,' he told me. When I reached home, I found my granddaughter coughing. She had coughed continually for two days but his father didn't seem to care. What could I do? I sold the fertiliser to buy her medicine. I planted the seeds without fertiliser, and so the harvest was poor," he posed thoughtfully. "The young man means well to us. Unlike our leaders, he is practical, but we are simply obstinate, only seeing through our blurred lenses. If we had only two Vincents in Mayenga, we could be miles ahead of where we are."

Finally, Millie was upbeat and confident as she stood on the podium before the crowd and enumerated her works in Mayenga. She was sharply dressed in a black suit and a matching white neck scarf. She looked immaculate. She did not appear disturbed by the disparaging rumours, and was full of praises for Vincent. "He made me reach the village and mobilize the women towards the Water Project. He has a great heart for you. He has provided leadership from the front and he is a mind beyond our recognition. The only reward you can give him is to support and ensure his projects succeed. This is for your good and betterment. The women of Mayenga, your contributions have lessened your loads. Going down to the falls for water is history. We now have no water-borne infections in Mayenga. I urge you to take your lives to the next level. The secrets are within you: your values as a community and a culture you create. We shall always be there to give you a helping hand," she concluded her speech with incessant applause from the crowd.

As an appreciation of her excellent work, the Mayenga Water Project management committee recognised her with a certificate and decorated her with traditional regalia, a sign that she was an elder in Mayenga, thus acknowledging her as one of their own.

The county public health officer (CPHO) and the officers from National AIDS Control Programme (NASCOP) were next in the dais. In the recent past, Mayenga had been hit by calamities and lost several people. There were no clear explanations to the deaths, but accusing fingers were pointing to acts of witchcraft, evil spirits roaming in the village or curses. Often, family members consulted witch doctors and diviners who gave them all forms of advices and remedies. Solutions ranged from unearthing and exorcising hidden 'witches' from the sick persons' compounds, giving sacrifices to appease and tame the tormenting spirits, and as a last solution when these were not yielding, the sick persons were taken to hospitals, usually in pathetic states. Soon, the patients died. In a bout of anger, many neighbours had resorted to hatred, mudslinging and open fights over the deaths. However, word was rife that HIV/AIDS (Human Immunodeficiency Virus/Acquired Immune Deficiency Syndrome) was responsible for the deaths. Many of those who had died had similar signs and symptoms. They were weak, emaciated and slowly, but painfully wasted away.

The county public health officer and the National aids Control Programme officers had earlier visited the village to sensitise the people on the plight of the disease. The perception of the village was that the disease was of the town dwellers, *ugonjwa wa mji,* the cursed ones, or as a result of witchcraft and evil spirits. So, the theme of the field day could not be complete without sensitising Mayenga on the dangers of HIV/AIDS. "People should come out and know their HIV status and be equipped with knowledge and vital health information about the disease and its damaging consequences," the CPHO said. Health information was disseminated through pamphlets that advocated for public awareness and behavioural changes. Free condoms were distributed to adults as a preventive measure against the spread of the HIV infection, other sexually transmitted infections and against unwanted pregnancies. People were enlightened on family planning as a means to stem large family burdens.

At question time, Morwabe shot up, and with his hand held to his chin, shook his head vigorously. He wondered why the government had decided to give a free ticket to people to misbehave by giving them condoms. He asked, "How can a person eat a sweet with its wrappers? Of what value would the sweet be? And you say a man can be operated on to plan his family?" he posed.

"The procedure is known as vasectomy for a man and tubal ligation for a woman. For a man, it's a simple surgical procedure compared to a woman, but it's optional," the CPHO informed. "There are other methods one can use as a measure of family planning, depending on their suitability and medical advice."

"You say, a man should do family planning, be operated on like a teaser bull and still go home to be a man in his house?" he queried amidst loud laughter from the crowd. Again, Morwabe shook his head, clicked and in his distinctive pessimism walked away from the meeting. "That is unheard of. Family planning is for women. Men, don't allow yourselves to be fooled," he comically shouted as he left. "The witches of Mayenga will ensure all your children are dead, knowing very well you're a castrated bull. You will neither remarry a woman with children to spearhead your name as the same witches here would have ensured all your cows are dead too. With no bride price, you are completely done."

Such were the stereotypical pessimisms that left the officers in tears and the crowd in rib cracking laughter, but affirmed that Mayenga was indeed obstinate.

Chapter Sixteen

Senta was a troubled man. The last time he was in Mayenga he had a bitter quarrel with Anna. The cause of their exchange was the sight of fresh wounds all over her body. For the second time, he noted, Anna had questionable fresh marks of incisions on her body, with old blotches still evident, leaving her brunette skin speckled with darkened spots. He had confronted her and sought an explanation for this, but Anna had rudely brushed him aside, terming his inquiry an intrusion into and snooping on her privacy. He was a man, she said, who didn't understand Mayenga at all. That marked the origin of their bitter exchange of words. In retaliation, she called him all kinds of names: an animal, a beast, a dog, a prostitute and good for nothing idiot. The abuses were too much to bear for a man in his house. He couldn't afford to complete his weekend in such a tense environment. In a rage, Vincent had stormed out of the house in a huff without telling her where he was going, entered his vehicle and driven back to the city. That was on a Saturday morning, barely a day at home.

In his office, he sat on his swivel chair in deep thought. As always, music on his laptop played some soft lyrics. He spent a lot of time checking the nearly endless play list for his favourite songs and replayed them repeatedly. His eyes were sunken and bloodshot with his breath smelling of beer. He had spent the previous night in a pub till morning, draining bottle after bottle of beer until he had no cash left in the pocket. He had gone for more from a nearby automated teller machine (ATM) and continued drinking all alone till morning. He left the pub direct to his office. He didn't understand why he was doing this, but his heart was troubled, and for a while, beer provided a temporary escape route from frustrations.

The room was cold and the workload had dwindled. He had few clients, as potential ones did not appear to take him seriously. Most of the times, he was out of the office in pubs, drinking and the office was largely run by his secretary, Nyambura. Even then, he did not appear to care as he felt sick inside, and had lost all that he had lived for, most of all Anna and his dignity as husband.

He had not travelled home for eight months. It was the longest he had ever been away from home and his family. He appeared angry, bitter, lonely and disconnected from life. His whole body twitched and ached. The realisation that his wife, Anna, the woman he loved so much, that he had been willing to go the extra mile to see her secure and comfortable, was actually a witch or consulting witch doctors behind his back, disturbed him. Further, she had lost all respect for him as a husband, and she could call him a good-for-nothing idiot, a dog and an animal, among other vulgarities.

"My skin hasn't felt the warmth of another body for long. It is now almost a year of disconnection with Anna. I feel miserable, lonely and hollow inside," he muttered to himself. He sighed deeply and seemed insecure. "I've tried hard. But I can't understand the people or Anna. Being away from home for this long can make even the most abstinent take a hard look at themselves. It can smarten one, make one adventurous and try to understand things one would never have understood," he talked to himself.

"Nyambura," he called out softly as he swung in his swivel chair.

Nyambura, his secretary, strode into his office from the reception in quick steps. She was in a fashionable black suit and a matching white blouse. "Yes sir. Did I hear you call me?"

"No, I didn't. Oh yes I did," Senta appeared grossly confused. "Take a seat, please." Senta motioned her to the clients' seat opposite him.

"You say you schooled at the university."

"Yes I did, but I've to do what is available for now."

"University chicks are choosy, love being stylish and smelling good," Senta snooped gently with a light beam on his face.

"That was then, my boss. Today, the scenario is different. There is no money to make one stylish."

"In the interview, you indicated that you're married. Am I right?"

"I had a boyfriend," Nyambura replied sheepishly.

"Where is he now? You live together?"

Nyambura reminisced, "I dated my boyfriend for about four years and we were a perfect match. So I thought. He was witty, humorous and we had many things in common. We toured the whole of Kenya. We had a son before I discovered the other side of him. He had a family in his rural home that was not aware of my existence. It was too much for me. We were too crowded, so I chose to live alone." she answered with a sediment voice.

"If I may intrude again, how do you meet your basics with the salaries we pay, given the escalating cost of living in the city?"

That was the best question from an employer. It meant something good. "I survive by the grace of God. To be precise, a chick can't go hungry when she knows her powers," Nyambura smiled candidly. "Also, boss, allow me to intrude."

"You're allowed," Senta replied in a haggard voice.

"Are you sick or something," she asked in a gentle and caring voice. "Of late, you've lost your enthusiasm. You look tired and not the boss I knew who was visionary, full of energy and took his work with exceptional zeal. As your secretary, trust me. I mean well, and my duties are to ensure that my boss carries out his work with diligence. That way, my job is secured too."

All of a sudden, Senta became more alert. Even his secretary had noted the mess in his life. He felt the pinch in his heart. "Nyambura, I must admit a few wrongs are breaking me. I'm a lonely man. I feel sick inside, and a longing for companionship. I had a loving family until I couldn't understand it. Like you, I'm all alone." He slumped into his seat with his eyes closed. Nyambura looked at him thoughtfully with sympathy written on her face. When he opened his eyes, tears streamed out in tandem to his cheeks. Nyambura took her white handkerchief from her bag, walked to his seat, sat on the edge and wiped the tears patting and massaging his back gently. "Don't cry my dear. I'll revamp you. I'm here for you," she said comfortingly in a sediment voice.

That marked the genesis of a rendezvous and exciting affair between Nyambura and Senta. It took them places where they could never have been together. They drank the latest brands, ate their best meals, danced and slept in silent night beds. That transcended a period of four years, before Nyambura passed on after a long illness bravely borne. Senta wept for her death, but his own health was in doubt. He was frequently in and out of hospital from bouts of malaria, typhoid, pneumonia and even diarrhoea. His finances went down, and with Nyambura's exit, his law firm lacked clients, and soon went under.

Chapter Seventeen

The witches of Mayenga had decided to have a field day. So it was said. They had ganged up to torment the village through their secret and wicked activities. Unlike before, hardly a season passed without new deaths. Many deaths were as a result of long illnesses or by what was termed as "eating well" or "overeating". Long illnesses, the hospitals said were as a result of cancers due to smoking cigarettes or liver cirrhosis caused by taking too much spirits. But the locals couldn't swallow the 'lies'. They said. "Food", as the illicit liquors were termed, couldn't just kill one like that. An act of witchcraft, roaming evil spirits or curses must have driven one to over-drink and wander in the frequently raging and boisterous rainstorms, which dug gullies on their paths and swept couples downhill. The information was gathered during the frequent funerals as people wailed, blaming all sorts of reasons for the deaths. Further, causes of deaths, the hospitals explained, were attributed to tuberculosis, amoeba, pneumonia and malaria, as a result of HIV/AIDS complications. But these ones too were mere reasons, they said, and the underlying causes were attributed to the same reasons. "How can diarrhoea or typhoid kill a person who drinks treated water of Mayenga? And if so, what was the need of treating it? Who knows when witches scheme evil and strike?"

With poverty ravaging the village, the treatments of choice were to consult diviners or witch doctors who could understandably offer solutions in three-piece treatments. They divined, prescribed herbal concoctions and exorcised the roaming spirits and "witches." So, as the demand for their services rose, the number of the diviners and witch doctors multiplied. Others arrived from afar and placed their billboards on roadsides, advertising their endless pros and received ready clients.

Infant mortality was at an all-time high. Most births were carried out by midwives, but some midwives who were rumoured to have bad omens, evil eyes, or said to be witches were silently proscribed as birth attendants. The hospitals blamed the mortality rate on HIV/AIDS and poor nutrition.

The main mode of HIV transmission was heterosexual contact. NASCOP explained that the infection rate in Mayenga was one of the highest in the country and the world. The statistics ranged at twenty per cent for the most productive ages of fifteen to forty-nine. This age bracket, they said, was the engine and the workforce of the community. The World Health Organisation (WHO) estimated that ten per cent of pregnant women were living with the HIV virus. The disease was thus a health crisis, and affected all other sectors of society, robbing Mayenga of the resources on which human development and survival depended on.

Sensitisation about the transmission, prevention and other crucial information were put on posters, billboards in the market and on vernacular radio stations. In the past, HIV/AIDS peer training programmes had been launched in the village. Selected groups of villagers were trained as the "trainer of trainers" (TOTs) programme and served as resources for their peers. However, the scourge was only mentioned in whispers and largely stigmatised.

Even though there was an effort to disseminate information about the disease and the dangers it posed, on average, the level of knowledge was poor, distorted by gossipers, and compounded by stigmatisation and cultural beliefs. Despite the threat caused by the disease, people continued practising risky sexual behaviour that could lead to more infections. Cultural practices, such as traditional girl circumcision better known as female genital mutilation (FGM), widow inheritance, were seen as a way of life. Men jostled and fought to inherit a widow even before grass had grown on her husband's grave, and a boy was a man if he dated several girls. Teenage pregnancies were a common sight. The use of traditional healers, beliefs in witchcraft and curses as the cause of death were widespread and ingrained. Even with education, some still termed HIV/AIDS, a "disease of town" or of prostitutes, "travellers", those who "walked badly", or those who had discarded their customs, thus inviting curses upon themselves. The disease was loathed and surrounded by mysteries. The factual information on the ground was that the disease was like leprosy if indeed it existed.

Many who were HIV positive were unaware of their status. Unknowingly, many were spreading the virus and leading lifestyles which could contribute to its continued progression. Free mobile visiting, counselling and testing, facilities (VCT), and treatment programmes were launched. However, those who accepted that there was such a disease had a number of misconceptions about it. Many people refused to be tested out of fear of how they would be perceived by the community if they tested positive. Fear was exacerbated by widespread misconceptions about the transmission and prevention of it. One who tested positive could easily spread it to others by a mere handshake or sharing facilities. Thus the victims became shunned and isolated from the community.

NASCOP said that if behavioural change was not taken seriously, the disease would continue to ravage the village further, leading to an over-burdened health care system, disintegrated family structures, an increased number of orphans, disparaging poverty as a result of a weak, sick labour force, and ultimately a severe drainage of community resources. The economic growth of Mayenga would be paralysed.

HIV/AIDS had been fought through education and awareness campaigns since the scourge was declared a national disaster. The aim was to prevent new infections from taking place, to improve quality of life for HIV positive people, and to reduce stigmatisation and discrimination among those infected and affected. These were carried out at schools, market centres, bars, churches, and through Mayenga women's group. Discussions on transmission and prevention of it and other sexual transmitted infections (STIs) were featured. Facts about HIV/AIDS that assisted in dispelling a multitude of rumours and myths concerning the disease were made available through calendars, pamphlets and magazines. Films such as *"Silent Epidemic"* and *"Facing the Challenge"* were used as effective teaching tools. Drama and songs formed part of the teaching programmes. Skits on how the virus attacked the white blood cells and weakened the body causing eventual death were aired live in the village and the market centre. Condoms were distributed and demonstrations of their proper use performed. Each presentation was concluded with an intensive question and answer session.

The open-forum style allowed those in attendance to feel free to ask even the most sensitive of questions. "We have realized through our community involvement that a high level of ignorance still exists about the origin, transmission, and prevention of the disease."

This was voiced during question and answer sessions after education. "Now we are aware that the disease is not caused by witchcraft." Based on the questions, it was discovered that many beliefs, myths, pessimism and ignorance had compounded the spread of HIV. Myths about condoms that they had tiny holes through which the virus could pass, that they were for loose moral people, did not elicit intended pleasure and that they were unhygienic were demystified. A belief was that people infected with the HIV could rid themselves of the virus by passing it to virgins and strangers, or to as many people as possible through repeated unprotected intercourse and more misconceptions were dispelled and replaced with facts about the virus.

By the end of the sessions, many villagers were eager for more information about the disease they were now aware of that was robbing them of their loved ones. Males and females left the venues enthusiastic about the new information. Some walked home fearful and distances apart. Some took it as a holistic work of salvation. Sadly, risky sexual behaviours dropped insignificantly partly due to cultural beliefs, and the number of eager people waned with time.

However, some villagers decided on what to do with the knowledge they had gained from the programmes and how it could best benefit Mayenga. With some input from NASCOP, they came up with ideas to distribute this knowledge and visit the sick ones at home. Women were particularly eager to implement the lessons learned.

Chapter Eighteen

Elder Gesaku held his glass of illicit beer high. He muttered some incoherent words of prayer and then poured some of it onto the ground. "This one is for you, the ancestors who preceded us. This land and everything on it are yours. Don't lead us into trenches, lead us onto slippery grass as people will see us and hold our hands home. Don't blind our eyes or break our legs, ankles or bones. Don't tamper with our brains and our health as I've bribed you in time with this food."

The other elders who sat with him in a semicircle concurred with his prayers by nodding their heads and said, "*ebe bo*, may it be so."

"We're the organs that rule Mayenga. We advise the chief on matters of the community and what goes on here," elder Gesaku continued. "And I've no reason as the chief elder to doubt that we haven't done well. We solve land disputes among brothers. One who doesn't respect the boundaries set and marked by elders is cursed. We tell them so, and fine them a little for our legs and mouths, doing errands and talking for Mayenga." He closed his eyes and swallowed half of the contents in the glass and continued. "We mete discipline to a woman who doesn't respect our customs. She has to bring a goat from her home to be cleansed. No one can pay us for what we do. Only God," he concluded with finality.

"We're here today," elder Nyanchoka took over, "for the good of Mayenga. Before the end of the day, we shall have contributed to the future of Mayenga, in kind. Though the government is tough on this 'food' we're taking," he pointed to the illicit brew, "we must allow Kemunto to sell it so that she can feed and educate her children. It's the only way we can pay back to her departed husband who was generous to us all. Every time he was in the village from his work, he was kind. He ungrudgingly showered us with lots of beer. I never missed a cigarette or two. God rest his soul in peace amongst the spirits," he shook his head for a moment. "But the evil ones were envious when he brought stones to lay the foundation for his house. He didn't live to spend a night in it. You can see some sand and stones waste away in the yard." He pointed to a heap of sand and stones on the side. "As if that was not bitter enough, his last born child followed him even before grass had grown on his grave. And they blamed it on the disease, yet we all know he didn't 'walk badly'. He was an upright man." He spat out voluminous saliva. "And our boys, some who are supposed to be his sons, brought shame by fighting to break the pinnacle of his house and 'fence' his homestead. Culturally, who is entitled to fence the homestead?" he asked hitting his chest hard. "It's me, his brother who is permitted by our customs to do so, even if Kemunto is half my age," he answered himself.

"Kemunto is a good woman," Gesaku praised her. "She never fails to give her liquor tips. Unlike the others in the village, she brings it herself very early before I wake up. Sometimes, I refuse and ask her to buy salt for the children. She is a piece of a good fruit."

It was evening and Kemunto was not at home. Many people had congregated in her home to take the illicit brew. They sat in several groups, with some of them visibly drunk, singing and talking incoherently. She was a known brewer and sympathetic eyes had given her a free licence against the chief's order of brewing and selling the illicit drink, in order to feed and raise her children. For the sake of 'tranquillity' the chief turned a blind eye. Mamu, Kemunto's first-born daughter, who was barely fifteen, was busy serving other customers.

"She sells like her mother. See. I'll order a round for you." Elder Nyanchoka called out for a round of beer. Mamu, who was serving other customers rushed to serve the elders. She filled a plastic bottle with illicit brew from a container and gently requested for payment. Elder Nyanchoka paid her and she left to serve a group of youth a distance away. "See," elder Nyanchoka called the others to attention. "It was the other day she was crawling. Now she is a woman with bulging buttocks and tummy. Who can take me back to my youth when I had the energy and could run and gather like a sow?" he laughed at his joke.

The chief had worked so hard to eradicate the illicit liquor in the village, which wasted a lot of time for the villagers and was blamed for all kinds of crimes and ill health, but it had cost him a name. Quietly, he was loathed and feared in the village for going against the grain and failing to understand it. Many thought his actions were meant to punish them and make their lives miserable. Even the elders, who he closely worked with and trusted to be responsible, misinterpreted and misrepresented him. "The chief must understand that we elders take this stuff because we have to be close to the people and pass time. I'm old, and this is not the time I can break my back in the gardens," one elder spitefully remarked. "As for the youth, they can take a little so long as they don't disturb anybody. Even our ancestors took the stuff, and yet their blood flows in our veins."

It was getting dark when Kemunto arrived at home from the market with a bag of sweet potatoes for supper. There was noise and commotion in her home caused by a group of brawling youth. The elders were a distance away ready to take flight as they were on on your marks position with their walking sticks in their hands and watched the youth tear into each other's throats. As usual, they were not ready to stand as witnesses to the fight or be caught in the brawl. "Let them fight," one elder said. "Tomorrow, they will call us to separate them, and give us 'bananas' to reconcile and unite them. That is our job as elders."

"A council of elders without cases to solve has no men to cause troubles," elder Nyanchoka qualified his statement. "Look! That is why we're elders. People must see our importance and pay us a little for uniting them."

The elders appeared to enjoy as the boys punched each other. "Look! That one punches like his late father," another elder said. "The late would never have thrown a punch if he was going to miss a target. Look! Look! Paw! Paw! c'mon. That was a wonderful punch. His is a real warrior of Mayenga!"

"Tomorrow, be sure we shall have work of 'separating' and 'uniting' them," elder Nyanchoka said. "The short one is too ferocious than the tall one and for that, he will give us more 'soup' for our work."

The cause of the fight was not clear until one braved it and shouted, "You've no shame! No respect, you bastard son of a bitch!" the tall youth insulted the shorter one. "Mamu is mine. I come here because of her and you know it. You knew her through me, but now you want to snatch her from me. No way! I'd rather die." It took the effort of the other youth to separate them. Then, they left for home in separate directions, each with his group, exchanging vulgar words.

Mamu was peeping through a window watching them tear into each other. Kemunto was lost for words when she heard Mamu being mentioned. She heavily threw the load on her head to the ground. Mamu was fourteen and in class eight. Kemunto was working hard to feed her children and raise fees for her and other siblings single-handedly as a widow. And these boys could not sympathise with her situation, but were busy spoiling her underage daughter. She pondered. "Uuui! We drink the same waters and write the same funeral book! What curse are you bringing to my house? Who can teach you manners?"

Momentarily, Kerongo, her first-born son staggered in demanding for food. "I want to eat!" he demanded.

"When did you start taking beer, you black porcupine? Am I your wife to demand food from?" Kemunto took a cooking stick and ran after him. Kerongo exited through the window into the dark night, dodging the stick that fell a step behind him. That evening, nobody ate a meal in the home as the situation was too tense to cook. Worse still, many customers took off without settling their liquor bills.

The next morning Kemunto had too much in her head. She wanted to make a report to the chief that her son and daughter, who she was working so hard to feed and raise fees for single-handedly, had grown too long horns for her to be able to dehorn. But she couldn't gather enough courage to face the chief. Several times, the chief had warned her against brewing and selling *changaa*. So, she reasoned, he would not listen to her. Instead he would take the opportunity to admonish her for failing to heed his advice. Gesaku would demand his fee before he listened to her problems. Nyanchoka had brought her several glasses of sugar with an aim to win her, but she had no strength to face the old lad who had little manners, though she had no qualms about him. "Is he still not capable of bringing sugar without these loathsome demands?" she reasoned. Instead, she chose to talk to her daughter, who she found vomiting behind the house.

"Tell me, Mamu, what's the matter?" Mamu had been vomiting in the morning for two consecutive days, and Kemunto was alarmed. Mamu kept quiet and instead started scribbling on the ground using her toe, thus forcing Kemunto to take a stick to get the information out of Mamu's head. This was her preferred way of disciplining her children. "You went to the hospital yesterday and you didn't come back with a card. Yesterday, boys were fighting in my compound because of you. Your horns are growing too long! I need to break some of them in time," she screamed menacingly. "Had your father been around, he would have taught you a lesson." Mamu tried to escape but Kemunto was faster. She held Mamu's dress and pulled her to the house and sat her on the bed. "Now tell me, where is the medicine from the health centre?" she held her stick threateningly. "You must give it to me before I strangle you with my bare hands and forget I ever delivered a daughter called Mamu in a night."

Mamu fetched a card from her school bag. Its heading was boldly inscribed, "MAYENGA MATERNITY CLINIC" and her name, Mamu Nyabwororo, was inscribed below it. It was a familiar card and as a mother, she had been issued one at the clinic. Kemunto studied the card thoughtfully for some time. She could not believe that her fourteen-year-old daughter was soon to be a mother. In her mind, Mamu was her pearl. She was the opener of her womb and as a mother she had endeavoured to provide and teach her on the path of life. She had wanted to do all within her means to provide for her education and secure her future, even in the absence of their father. She always encouraged her children to work hard and told them that their father was on a long journey and would only come back if they excelled in school. And for that very reason, she had disobeyed the chief's orders to brew and sell *changaa*. Now, she was at a loss. "Of the boys fighting last night, who's responsible for your pregnancy," she inquired politely amidst tears.

"The tall one," Mamu replied shyly.

"Did he force you?" she probed.

"He cheated me," Mamu answered.

"How did he cheat you?" Kemunto queried sarcastically.

"He told me that he would marry me," she replied.

"Uuui! My God, come down now. Hear me! My sweat has come to nothing. That beast of a monkey with a mouth of calabash cheated you, you tin-legged thing!" she screamed with her hands holding her head and momentarily bit her fingers. "No wonder the imbecile of the witch was ever seen here holding an empty glass! I must tell the chief and his father." She rushed to fetch water from a drum outside her house to wash her legs. "Though I know the father will rejoice and be proud that his son has proved his manliness by messing my daughter," she muttered. "He will be happy that more suckers are sprouting from his stem, yet he cannot buy even a napkin for the little one."

The wash basin she had recently bought was missing. There were several broken glasses and the benches in the shade where the boys were fighting. She stood akimbo and counted her losses. Now with a drunkard son hardly out of school and a pregnant daughter, she was at a loss for words. "The chief says I should stop this and embark on farming or something else, but the elders are happy with me. They say my brew is the best in Mayenga. It's good for their thirst, and they "protect me" for a small token. On good days I make some money, but on bad ones, I'm left counting losses, particularly when the administration police (APs), who don't understand my plight, raid my house. The chief will only laugh at me and be sterner. I've seen diviners to have him soften his stance on me, but his heart doesn't appear to yield. The witches of Mayenga who killed my husband have completely turned his heart against me, and proceeded to bewitch my children. Who doesn't know that my husband's beer was secretly laced with some deleterious concoction so that he could die a slow death and they could blame it on the disease. During his burial, the chief himself didn't mince his words. He said pointing his finger at me, 'You're now on your own. If you don't toe the line, the spirits of Mayenga won't spare you, even if you're now a widow.' By saying so, he gave the witches a free ticket to torment me. Who will wipe my tears? Ooh God! God of the widows and orphans! Come down right now." she wailed hysterically. "After all, a child is not a bad thing and is a blessing from God. Mamu isn't the first one in Mayenga to have a child out of wedlock! Once it's born, I'll hold and dote on it like this."

Chapter Nineteen

Several churches had established their bases in Mayenga and each had pulled a sizeable following from the village. They held crusades in the market and did rounds in the village to win more souls into their flocks. Some had even erected buildings through the efforts of the villagers. Almost every home was affiliated to one church or another.

Some sects had found their way in as means of offering solutions to the people's problems. Mecha's faith was seen as one of them. Though fewer men attended the services, their children and wives gave their homes intransigent sectarian identities. This was evident on weekends, when even those who never attended church services took a day off to clean their compounds, take a rest from any laborious duty and relax in the market or in *changaa* dens, chatting. During crusades, drunken villagers came out to listen to the messages of salvation and dance with disregard to the choruses and hymns of Christian music belted from heavy percussions. They merely enjoyed the music, but occasionally in a strange fit, some were converted, leaving the crowd mesmerised. "God has come down and saved a soul," the men of God said in such scenarios.

Converts met regularly and shared the word of God: to nurture, build, and look out for each other. They exalted principles of bearing one another's burdens, being kind and hospitable to each other, honour, service, respect, admonishing and confessing sins, forgiveness and acceptance. They preached about the grace of God and against sinning. Prayer groups, home Bible studies, and sometimes just being together sharing and having fun formed means of pastoring and encouraging the spread of the word of God in Mayenga. They say a church that prays together stays together; the church that sings together clings together, and one that shares, cares for one another. "As believers in Christ, you are never alone. You are a citizen of the Kingdom of God, with many others," the pastors preached. "And the burdens of the earth will be uplifted." Witches causing miseries were seen as the works of the devil, Satan, and believers were told they would trudge through snakes and scorpions unscathed. However, most of the activities were centred on converting souls and evangelism, irrespective of their welfare. Some villagers saw it as a holistic approach and a protagonist against their traditional culture.

Believers continued to languish in abject poverty, ignorance, diseases and outdated beliefs, lacking in essentials and afflicted by the tribulations of Mayenga like everybody else. All types of vices continued to flourish and many people groaned under these burdens.

Many people appeared to be drawn to churches out of what they could gain at the end, rather than the doctrine of salvation. Some saw it as a place of worship where people could just belong. More often, the congregation studied the Bible, listened to the preaching, and come evening, some were seen drunk, caught in brawls or bickering with their neighbours over trivialities. Behind the scenes, it was said, they sought for solutions to their problems from diviners and witch doctors. Those who were bold and zealous were left more alone, ashamed, or condemned. People pointed at Mecha, and questioned the role of the church in the community's well-being. He had shunned the community and he was lonely for the cause. "Is this what Christ says believers will be known by?" they questioned: "To be lonely? Not to be understood? Has the church made Mecha and Moraa lonely, ashamed, verified and rejected by society?"

The resources were becoming overwhelmingly depleted as the population increased, and the livestock and crops were perennially failing. Outdated farming approaches were the chosen way of life. And the humanitarian assistances for the followers were the word of God. "How do they expect us to listen to the Good News on empty and rumbling stomachs? From our sick beds?" people questioned. But there was a ready answer from the churches. "There is an underlying spiritual darkness here!" they preached, "that ensured a state of poverty and distress in the village. Only salvation would pull you out of this state of affairs."

Despite their vigorous crusades to the village, the churches had scarcely created an impact in Mayenga, in the economy, their culture and spirituality.

Shortly, an evangelical mission set a base at Mayenga, and it was seen like the other churches. Its aims were to preach the word of God and teach Mayenga to fish its own fish. They wanted to develop local resources too in order to improve the quality of life in Mayenga. Then, they could have a platform to spearhead the gospel. They mobilized the community and church leaders to identify resources and resource needs and to set out ways of transforming Mayenga. Most of the resources needed to support these already existed within the village. The village had land, water, labour, electricity and many others.

The mission started with establishing a free health centre in the village for the village to win their trust and confidence that indeed they cared for their welfare too. Many people came to be treated. Some patients came in after their visits to the witch doctors and diviners had not yielded results. They were treated and they recovered. Word spread that the mission health centre could cure any disease, and streams of patients flowed in overwhelmingly. The mission took the opportunity to treat and evangelize to them. It highlighted the dangers of lifestyle, and brainstormed on behavioural and attitudinal change to survive the challenges of the times. HIV/AIDS education was offered too and was demystified to dispel the multitude of rumours and myths. Prevention of transmission of HIV from mother to child services (PMTCT) was also offered at the clinic.

The mission began to visit homes, make friends, take time to listen and learn what the people believed in, and what held them back. They realized that the village had several beliefs and myths. They also realized that whatever they did had a reason and underlying factors, and that there were under-utilised resources available in Mayenga to sustain development. The people were hard working and intelligent, but lacked the leadership capacity, training and immediate resources to change their lives. People would gather around the missionaries and discuss freely their plight and fears, and even map their way forward, but in the end their eyes were expecting. They needed transformation, and not transactional hand-outs, to meet their needs and transform their own lives, the mission concluded.

For these reasons, the mission developed a leadership model for the village. Its role was to identify community needs, sensitize and mobilize the people, and oversee poultry production in partnership with the church. It provided training, day old chicks, feeds, treatment and the marketing service while the farmers were to provide labour and structural facilities for the chicken. The programme worked marvellously. This again created a platform to preach, teach the principles of family life, parenting, integrity and leadership. Mayenga began to change as the youth took an active role selling the eggs to other markets for a living, and keen ones were challenged to start their own poultry and dairy farming.

A self-sustaining microfinance programme was introduced from which one could borrow and pay back at a reasonable interest rate. The criteria were to identify a project and initiate it with the assistance of the mission, which assisted in credit appraisal, extension and monitoring services.

The village agreed that qualified leadership, which they had all along lacked, was the key to any tangible development. Initially, leadership was not seen as a platform to serve but as twist and take-it-all game. The perception was that aspiring leaders were able to bribe their ways to the "granaries" to share the spoils. They started to entrust the village leadership to people who were perceived to have the integrity and the skills necessary to articulate their mission, vision and implement their agendas. An effective village committee consisting of church members and trusted people was formed. Kundi was chosen as their chairman. Their mandate was to oversee their projects, be the links to the mission, influence change, recruit new members to the programmes, determine who qualified to be in the programmes and ensure that the programme's guidelines were adhered to. They were also mandated to monitor the activities of the village and report to the members and the mission.

Gradually, a difference in how people spent their time could be noted compared to the past. There was less desperation. Many families had simply lacked the energy and knowledge to keep their gardens, properly store food and cook the variety of foods necessary for good nutrition. Disease incidences went down and people saw the need to identify serious illnesses and seek medical attention in time, as opposed to seeking solutions elsewhere. Children started to attend schools regularly as many parents started to appreciate the need for education and were now empowered to meet the costs.

Many appreciated the role played by The Mission in changing perceptions towards their lives. Most of all, they had needed the knowledge and hope. And during the weekends, a stream of followers attended the service at The Mission with their Bibles and hymns. People could be heard talking, "God called the mission to address our problems." Volunteers from the mission assumed responsibility for daily visits to the homes in distress. Areba's home hosted many churches which streamed in to comfort the family and pray for Senta who had been taken ill. Their gesture was lauded.

The approach worked well, giving the mission a strong footing in Mayenga. However, it was going to take time for Mayenga to change its ways of life, which had become so entrenched over time.

Chapter Twenty

Inside Senta's house were Senta, his mother, Nyaboe, his wife, Anna, and his aunt Moige. They stayed by Senta comforting and nursing him. Moige sat on a stool holding her chin, looking disturbed and thoughtful, having spent countless nights comforting her sister Nyaboe to feel warm and brave the calamity that was at hand. Anna gently massaged Senta's back with a warm towel as he lay in bed lifeless and covered to his waist with a white sheet. His whitish, sunken eyes were staring blankly into space. Though the weather was cold, he was coughing repeatedly and sweating profusely. Senta had been discharged from hospital a week earlier. He had been given medicine to take at home. He needed to eat well; a balanced diet to regain his health, the doctors had advised. Anna pounded some tablets into fine powder and stirred them into a light paste using water as Vincent's throat and mouth had severe wounds. He could not swallow solid things.

In the shade outside the house, some people sat, consulting in low voices. Since Senta was discharged from hospital, the home had experienced an influx of visitors who came to inquire about his condition, wish him quick recovery and keep the family warm and brave.

"The doctors said my son is infected. Infected with AIDS! I can't believe the lies." Nyaboe was in a state of denial. "And the witches of Mayenga have made the rumour a song in the village and the market, to cover their own wicked trails. How can my son be infected, when he doesn't 'walk badly' like other men?" Nyaboe muttered to herself. "Didn't Gwako confirm my fears? This village! This village of Mayenga! What's its best bribe? He bribed them by giving them clean drinking water and hand-outs. Now they have no appreciation. Whoever betrothed me and made me agree to be married amongst witches messed me up. He dug my grave earlier, in broad daylight as I watched."

Nyaboe was dressed in a red *kanzu* and an overflowing black coat. Her head was tied in a black scarf exposing a veil of grey hairs. She was obsessed, praying to and appeasing the gods and the spirits of the land that she believed were tormenting her son Vincent. At the same time, she was admonishing the powers of the witches who empathized with her by day but tormented her by night. "If it is our god, *engoro,* whom we have offended and isn't pleased with us, I plead for forgiveness," she supplicated with her raised hands and her eyes welling in tears. "No sacrifice is small for you. We shall slaughter the fattest bull for you come the next season when crops have ripened. If it is our ancestors who are unhappy with us for some reasons, we shall give the best sacrifice and dance once the harsh season is over." She turned and held Senta's hand and prayed, "and if it's your grandfather, my son, who you stayed with like a body-flea till he left us that early morning as the sun rose without a word of farewell, but we haven't "brought him home" and into the house, have mercy on us as my son faithfully lit fire in your hut, and at no time did he offend you. He devotedly ran errands for you to fetch your tobacco and delivered your messages to the elders on his quick legs. We salute you. We shall slaughter the bull we have set aside, brew the most potent beer for you and bring you into the house, so that you shall always be a silent visitor and partaker within our midst. We shall put fire in the hearth for you to warm yourself, and the ashes shall be sprinkled on your grave to signify warmth. You shall be a step away to hear and protect us. For the world is bad; full of bad eyes and spirits ready to devour us. We shall bring you together with other ancestors who now you commune with in a land sealed from our eyes."

As she implored, Moige and Anna administered the medicine. Moige fetched some herbal fluid from a bottle and gave it to Senta. "You will heal, my son. Gwako has assured us. Take it," she pleaded. Senta swallowed it with a grimace on his face as he faintly stared at them.

Outside the house, there were many villagers who had come to inquire about Senta's condition. They all appeared to blame the witches of Mayenga. "They have no mercy or shame," one villager said. "How can they torment the only water they drink? The only eye that can see in the village? And the disease can't be seen in hospitals or respond to medicine."

"If his condition doesn't appear to improve by evening, I can go and fetch Gwako," another one offered.

"Gwako was here only yesterday, and he assured us that my son will feed back to recovery," Areba answered in a resigned voice. "This time the spirits had mercy on us. They demanded only a goat for his stomach and his legs for forest. That was more than a favour. Gwako said, the 'elephant' will eat all my wealth and leave me wretched, but in the end he will recover and I shall regain my wealth." He shook his head slowly. "This ailment is indeed an elephant that has haunted us. It has defied *mete anchogu*, herbal concoctions and Gwako appears desperately hapless."

Senta persevered all through his illness maintaining a lucid, rather passionate, but timid smile. When he had a bout of energy, he cracked jokes, asking about the Mayenga Water Project and how his children were faring. Sometimes, he hallucinated calling his friends by names and inviting them to see the Mayenga Water Project. He would call Millie to come and team up with him to ensure the water project succeeded. He would praise her energy, enthusiasm, professionalism and thank her for the job well done. He would call Nyamwanda and Mecha to join up with the rest of the community to tap the water, and he would affectionately ask his wife, Anna, to leave the things of the world and embrace God seriously. Those who heard him talk had all sorts of interpretations. Some said that Millie's love potion was still in his head, and others said that Nyamwanda and Mecha had travelled for him and cast a tougher spell on him.

Anna remained thoughtful. She dutifully nursed him and bore the brunt of moving him from bed to the sun, and then back to the house. She bathed him and fed him like a baby. When his condition worsened, Senta was taken to the county hospital under the advice of the county public health officer, who had been a constant visitor to the home.

Chapter Twenty-One

People thronged to the county hospital to see Senta, empathize with his family and wish him a quick recovery. They comforted and encouraged him. Villagers took turns to stay overnight with the family to comfort, encourage and keep them warm and brave. Mecha and Moraa were the only ones who were rare in the homestead. Theirs were a technical appearance, and even then they never inquired about his condition or suggested any remedy. The villagers sadly noted this fact. For the entire period Senta was hospitalised, they did not go to visit him there. A hospital, the couple said, was not a place for them, and they could not contravene their faith by going there.

Senta was admitted in the hospital for two months. The nights were uniquely cold and darker than usual. The crickets shrilled and an owl eerily hooted continually for the last week; the hospital lighting and other systems were frequently interrupted. It rained for days unabated, and regularly, the sky thundered in deafening roars with blinding lightning.

Senta laid lifeless in his hospital bed wasted to the bones. He had barely conversed for the entire period he was in hospital. One misty evening he looked at his mother and aunt Moige who were beside him. He stared at them for some time with glassy eyes and weakly called out, "Mother," he posed and coughed out imperceptibly. "Mother," again he muttered from the throat. His voice was hoarse and incoherently mystic. "Give me chicken soup."

"He is recovering. The injections and drugs are finally working," Nyaboe said to her sister Moige as they exchanged knowing glances.

"Let me fetch it from the canteen," Moige offered, fumbling to fetch a note from her purse. "Didn't Gwako assure us that he will eat well on his path to recovery? He must eat what the body demands to regain his health, strength and rebuild his muscles." She rushed out with a thermos flask leaving Nyaboe holding her son's head on her lap and massaging his back gently. Senta's body twitched and shivered. He had bold rashes all over his body.

"Mother, I've disturbed you. Give me porridge," Senta demanded again in a mumbled and distant voice. He was sweating all over his body. Gaping wounds in his mouth and throat, sores and red blotches on every part of his body had multiplied. He had not eaten a meal for days and had only survived on spoon-fed water and injection drips.

His mother reached to a thermos flask that contained millet porridge. It was hot. She poured it into a saucer to cool. When it was reasonably cold, she held his open mouth, and using a spoon, poured porridge directly into his oesophagus. He painfully swallowed, groaning. She forced more porridge into his mouth until the cup was half-full, but this time he clenched his teeth in evident excruciating pain and shook his head violently. Most of the liquid flowed out and down his bony cheeks.

"Mother," he weakly and incomprehensively called out again. "I've disturbed you." His distant eyes stared at her pathetically. "Hold my head. I will never forget you mother and aunt Moige. Where is Anna?" His drowsy, glassy eyes slowly moved towards the rustic wall facing the window and the peeling ceiling. He coughed loudly as if to remove a lump of clot from his lungs. More porridge mixed with blood exited through the mouth and nostrils.

In the past few days, Senta's health had declined drastically even as he lay helplessly in the hospital. The blotched sores and wounds all over his body had doubled by day and oozed pus. His mouth and throat had even larger open wounds. He was sweating profusely and coughed continually. He appeared to have lost the will to live and had less interest in things he once loved and enjoyed. He never inquired about his children or his water project that he had passionately initiated. He slept more and when he was awake, he was more preoccupied with spiritual matters and the destiny of man. His skin was cold, wrinkled, clammy and bluish in colour. His pulse and blood pressure were drastically low. At times he muttered unintelligible words. He disliked some visitors who came to see him in the hospital and would look sad and angry if one tried to sympathise with him. But he had immense fondness for his mother and aunt Moige. He hardly eliminated any refuse as the intestines had nothing. His eyes appeared whitish and glassy, with a distant stare-off into space as if in prolonged hallucinations. He had lost his appetite, but occasionally he could demand a soda or iced juice which he hardly took. "Mother, I need cold soda," he would call feebly with a forced grin that bore a masked contortion. He was very frail indeed.

On this particular day, Senta had a spurt of energy. He even joked and asked whether Gwako had been around, and if Mecha had cast his *nyachieni* into the inferno before he went to sleep. Moige hadn't returned with the soup.

"Do you feel me, my son," Nyaboe held his arm as he slept. Senta did not respond. She shouted out close to his ear. Still, he did not respond. His stare was glassy, fixed onto the ceiling. His breath was distant, far apart and more laboured with an occasional rattle from deep inside the chest. In a seizure his body twitched violently, and then he sighed heavily. He took his last breath as his heart beat retrogressed until there were no more beats. His body stiffened. The eye of Mayenga was closed to the world. The entire village of Mayenga was thrown into profuse mourning.

When Moige returned with a flask full of chicken soup, she saw a team of medics in white overcoats and stethoscopes hanging from their necks around Senta's bed frantically attending him. Nyaboe was pacing around the room, shaking her hands and wailing in elegies. "My kingpin is gone," she wailed:

1. *Eriso ria baba riatekire*
   Eriso ria baba riatekire
   Eriso ria Mayenga riatekire
   Obororo
2. *Rongori ya bekirwe echumbi*
   Rongori ya bekirwe echumbi
   Rongori ya bekirwe echumbi
   Yaa

Translated:

1. The eye of my mother has gone blind
   The eye of my mother has gone blind
   The eye of Mayenga has gone blind
   In grief
2. Salt has been put in Porridge
   Salt has been put in Porridge
   Salt has been put in Porridge
   Yaa

Nyaboe did not have to be told that Senta had closed his eyes to the world. She smashed the flask onto the floor as she wailed and screamed, and started to tear her clothes. Their endeavour had produced no fruits. The pain was not in the cost of his treatment, but the loss of a dear one. Indeed Gwako had foreseen his death. "There's no point of taking him to the hospital," he had advised. "Though the evil spirits have grown roots to the big waters, I shall try to uproot them and make them impotent from my house." "But," he had warned, "the evil ones have broken half of his back," Gwako had observed as he left the homestead in haste swaying his body to the dark night.

Chapter Twenty-Two

That chilly morning, before the sun rose, a sombre mood engulfed the entire village of Mayenga. There were soulful wails and screams as the village was thrown into profound mourning. Word had filtered in very early that morning that Senta was gravely ill, but the rumour was confirmed when Senta's mother and aunt Moige arrived home from the hospital very early with Senta's clothes and other belongings, profoundly wailing and screaming. "The eye of Mayenga has been forcefully gorged out. The lights have gone off. The taps have gone dry and the roads to Mayenga have been closed," they wailed mournfully in dirges.

Nobody could believe that Senta was no more. Grace ran from her house screaming with her sympathetic eyes welling in tears and sprawled on the muddy ground. "Anna, *ominto*, my sister, how will you manage all alone?" she wailed. "How will you bring up the children? Who will buy you sugar? Who will bring you salt?" she had a lesso tied around her loin. Anna was dumbfounded and was being resuscitated to life by sympathetic village women who stood by her, handy for any eventuality. The women's waists were wrapped with clothes, belts or sweaters.

Areba had had a horrible dream early that morning. A giant python had sleuthed into his bedroom through a vent and coiled itself around his neck as he slept in his room. He had woken up in time and a fierce fight with the beast ensued. He called and screamed calling Senta to come to his rescue, but Senta did not respond. Suddenly, he woke up panting and sweating, and as an extension of the dream, he heard screams and wails outside his house. He quickly leapt out of his bed and ran out. There were few people outside aimlessly pacing, running, wailing and crying. More people were streaming into his compound. When he saw his wife and Moige, he knew his son was no more.

"Where's my son," Areba inquired wailing acerbically. "They have killed my son. They have killed him. The eye of Mayenga has been forcefully gorged out," he wailed deafeningly in melodic elegy. "Death, what is your price to spare my son. Death! Look at me! Why me? Do I deserve this? A wretched idiot with neither a front nor a back? What wrong have I done to you or the village of Mayenga? Where're you hiding so that I can make use of my sword? Oh, my son," he emotionally wailed repeatedly, pacing from point to point and brandishing a double edged sword. "Is it because of the house he built for me? Or is it because of the waters he brought you, you jealous brutes. Who will dress me with a new shirt, and who will give life to Mayenga? Why couldn't you kill me, but spare my son? Why couldn't you leave him a cripple, but let him live for me to continue seeing him?"

"We have left him in the hands of God," Moige wearily informed him as Areba whistled in dirges. 'Go and fetch Gwako, Gwako the tough medicine-man.' "Senta is now resting with his creator and the ancestors. We have tried. Oh Porridge has mixed with salt. Milk has spilt onto the ground, and the pot has broken at the doorstep. The eye of Mayenga is blind." She wailed bitterly. "Why couldn't you have any mercy?"

Word spread quickly in the entire village and the market centre early that morning that Senta was no more. Shops were hurriedly closed, and those in their gardens threw down their tools and with fresh garden soils on their feet, ran screaming and wailing to Areba's home. Morwabe arrived blowing a large twisted horn with enthusiasm, whose echoes resonated across the land. Despite being next-door neighbours, Mecha and Moraa were among the last people to arrive at the homestead. They found people from miles away in the homestead, sobbing and screaming, wailing, and flashing fresh twigs. Some had even torn their clothes, exposing their chests. Mecha stood alone at a corner with one hand holding a huge wooden cross, and another holding his chin and wearing a sad and mournful face. He was in his trademark attire of black flowing gowns, a red cap inscribed with 'Almighty Almighty' and a huge red cross. He had a spotted greyish, long, unkempt beard. Though he did not wail or sob, he appeared very sad and concerned indeed. He was cheerless and seemed to have been touched by the death of Senta. However, his faith did not permit him to wail or shed a tear. "Man," he always said, "was from soil, and into soil, man shall return. Better wail for the living." His wife, Moraa, was dressed in the same manner, but with a smaller wooden cross, and was at a distance in a group of wailing women and frantically pacing and shaking her hands. She wore a mournful face and tried to wail, but no tears flowed out of her eyes.

In their distinctive manner, they left to their home as the senior elder, Gesaku, had calmed down the wailing crowd and summoned them to the shade for the funeral arrangements. Mecha and Moraa had nothing to do with non-believers who, they said, had gone astray and sinned against the Almighty Almighty.

Soon, loud voices of intermittent prayers, drums, songs and claps were heard from Mecha's house. As usual, the couple was typically binding and casting *nyachieni* into an inferno, where he would burn for ages, and invoking the Almighty Almighty to take control.

"This is Mayenga mourning a great loss," Kundi stood up and interrupted the senior elder as he led the drawing of the funeral preparations. "Mayenga's own eye is broken. A loved one who had done a lot for our people is no more." His voice rose in a crescendo and his eyes bitterly surveyed the crowd with welling tears rolling down his sunken cheeks. "Where is Character?" He asked authoritatively as drumming went on in Mecha's house. "Can it be that Mecha can't be with us here at this moment of grief?" he decisively asked. "Yet, he drinks the same waters from the tanks the departed painstakingly initiated?" His voice and body shuddered like a tremor and his skin turned pale. "If he died today, it would be the responsibility of Mayenga to bury him. He never bothered to visit the deceased in the hospital, even once. I watched him as he came in, and he didn't even bother to ask how our brother spent his last moments, or even shed a tear," he posed to swallow saliva.

Morwabe shot up with his horn in one hand and a walking stick in the other, and with his distinctive eloquence said, "We're all mourning a great man who brought us water and light. Can it be that Moraa can't find tears in her eyes, yet this man here can tear his own new shirt and leave his chest bare?" he gesticulated, pointing at Menge who was the village coordinator of the Mayenga Water Project. "What does Mecha or Moraa know about Senta's demise?" He halted in contemplation, pointing his walking stick at Mecha's house. "I remember Gwako's divinations." He reminisced loudly for the crowd to hear. "The witches were put there by ones not in this midst to guide the spirits to the home. Ones not in this meeting, but share water with the people of Mayenga are responsible. Why did he build such a house in the village, where there are so many evil eyes? They are driven by innate and shrewd jealousy, and now are seething and pissing in fear, invoking their powers not to be exposed and harmed. That is why they can't dare be in our presence,' Gwako had said."

Kundi interjected, "My own grade cow Senta, Senta's project, the first breed in Mayenga, was killed! It was bewitched in broad daylight and nothing happened." He shook his head even more vigorously as more tears welled in his eyes and rolled easily down his cheeks forming small streams.

There were protracted murmurs from the crowd. The youth who were aggressively charged had made a decision that no tongue could convince them to abandon. Like lightning, they bolted from the shade and sealed all the entrances to Mecha's house downhill. The couple was inside carrying on with their activities unaware of what was transpiring outside. The angry youth were armed with machetes, spears, sticks and axes, shouting and chanting as they crowded around the house. In the blink of an eye, Mecha and Moraa's house downhill was in flames with smoke and bluish flames bellowing up from the iron-roofed house. It razed quickly assisted by high speed winds. The chief and elders who were in the shade were astonished at the sizes of the flames and the scent of roast meat from the house.

Nyamwanda, the skins and hides' dealer stood, arms akimbo, and delightfully watched from the shade while Mecha and Moraa's house burned with yellow flames and smoke spiralled up to the sky. "Like a bull in a herd, a great man doesn't go down alone without some followers. Senta was indeed a great man," he remarked blissfully. "I'll now dry my skins and hides in Character's field. He had no cow or goat, and never in his life sold me a skin," he muttered to himself.

"Ooh my Lord, Jesus Christ of Nazareth, who was nailed on the cross with no sins. What's happening there?" the chief queried loudly as he shot up from his chair to have a better view of the scene. "Can someone tell me what is happening at Character's house?" With urgency, he commanded. "Obee! My job! What am I going to tell my bosses who are encapsulated in their offices and anxiously waiting for such reports?" He placed his hands on his forehead and trained his eyes to see clearly. "I can't see clearly or believe what is going on there, but heavy smoke is rising from the ground and a horrible stench is filling the air," he bellowed in astonishment. "What wrongs has Mecha done to the people of Mayenga to deserve this? Those who understand him well know he is a good man who wouldn't hurt a fly and minds only his business. His only undoing is that he is too engrossed in his faith!" he nervously yelled as he paced aimlessly watching the scene.

Many more people were streaming into Mecha's compound chanting war songs, some of them with dry wood and fresh twigs, adding them into the protuberant and rattling fire. Suddenly, a man razing in flames emerged through a burning window with a large wooden cross in one hand and screaming at the top of his voice for mercy. "Uuui! Please spare me! Ooh, Almighty Almighty, take control! The devil is cast on fire! *nyachieni* is the bad one!" He screamed loudly amidst choking smoke, with his face shiny dripping with sweat. He was followed by a woman in a black flowing garment carrying a smaller cross, engulf in flames and equally pleading for mercy, but she collapsed and fell at the razing window. Flying stones and all manner of objects hit Mecha onto the ground as he bolted out in flames. Then, the youth went after him, beat him with sticks and clubs, tied him with ropes and dragged him back into the raging fire. They were shouting and chanting, "Witch! Witch! Kill him! Burn him! Burn him." Then, he saw Morwabe, the acclaimed village rumour monger, struggle uphill with a huge log, heavier than himself, and precisely throw it into the brazen fire. He shouted at the top of his voice, "yesterday I slept hungry, and today I've not had a cup of tea." Typically, he stepped back, dusted his hands, and then with his arms folded on his chest, he eagerly watched the fire consume the log to the last splinter.

The chief, who remained in the shade throughout, was so terrified to go near the scene. He frantically paced and held his head in a mammoth of thoughts. Those who remained with him had to contend with his fidgeting and avalanche of questions: "Who? What? When? Why? And how?" Nobody could tell him what had transpired, though rumours were rife in Mayenga, and beyond that Mecha and Moraa were witches and were actually responsible for Senta's death.

My long-time favourite poem by an anonymous author is worth remembering today:

Don't quit

When things go wrong as they sometimes will,
when the road you're trudging seems all uphill.
When the funds are low and the debts are high,
and you want to smile, but you have to sigh.
When care is pressing you down a bit,
Rest if you must, but don't you quit.

Life is queer with its twists and turns,
As every one of us sometimes learns.
And many a fellow turns about,
When he might have won had he stuck it out.

Don't give up though the pace seems slow,
You may succeed with another blow.

Often the goal is nearer than
It seems to a faint and faltering man.
Often the struggler has given up,
When he might have captured the victor's cup.
And he learned too late when the night came down,
How close he was to the golden crown.

Success is failure turned inside out,
The silver tint of the clouds of doubt.
And you never can tell how close you are,
It may be near when it seems afar.
So stick to the fight when you're hardest hit,
It's when things seem worst that you mustn't quit.
And that's worth thinking about.

END